Rye had been prepa..... .... rain, and the warmth, ... the metal-box houses—but he hadn't really been prepared for Dad's being Governor . . . for his being so absolutely in charge . . .

There are other things that take Rye by surprise as he gets to know the island—the lizards that burn you if you touch them; the secret caves; the gods and their magic; the underground prison and the prisoner's daughter. And all the time people keep telling him how like his father he is.

Rye makes friends with Kris, an island boy, and together they explore the colony and try to find out its secrets, and the reasons behind all the disasters that are putting the very existence of the colony in jeopardy. But in facing up to the greatest threat of all, Rye has to choose where his loyalties lie, and discovers that being so like his father may not be such a bad thing after all.

Sally Prue has lived in Hertfordshire ever since she was adopted as a baby. When she left school she worked at the local paper mill before leaving to look after her two daughters. She now teaches the piano and the recorder. She started writing as a teenager when she discovered that inventing adventures is in some ways even more satisfying than having real ones. *Ryland's Footsteps* is her third novel for Oxford University Press.

Ryland's Footsteps

Other books by Sally Prue

Cold Tom
The Devil's Toenail

Ryland's Footsteps

Sally Prue

OXFORD
UNIVERSITY PRESS

OXFORD

UNIVERSITY PRESS

Great Clarendon Street, Oxford OX2 6DP

Oxford University Press is a department of the University of Oxford.
It furthers the University's objective of excellence in research, scholarship,
and education by publishing worldwide in

Oxford New York

Auckland Bangkok Buenos Aires
Cape Town Chennai Dar es Salaam Delhi Hong Kong Istanbul
Karachi Kolkata Kuala Lumpur Madrid Melbourne Mexico City Mumbai
Nairobi São Paulo Shanghai Taipei Tokyo Toronto

Oxford is a registered trade mark of Oxford University Press
in the UK and in certain other countries

British Library Cataloguing in Publication Data available

ISBN 0 19 271949 1

1 3 5 7 9 10 8 6 4 2

Typeset by AFS Image Setters Ltd, Glasgow

Printed in Great Britain by
Mackays of Chatham Ltd, Chatham, Kent

1

The walls closed in.
No, he thought, desperately, and kicked out as hard as he could.
But still the walls closed in.
They thrust him into exile.

He lay, stranded and helpless, and the mountainous creatures that inhabited this new world reached out for him, and they were hard and cold.

And he was helpless, utterly. They were so impossibly strong, and the light was blinding, bright, white. He screwed up his eyes against it. He would have turned away, except that the long struggle of his journey had left him so weak that he could hardly turn his head.

And now he was drowning: drowning, and lost, and cast away out of his world.

In fear and rage, he screamed.

This was a terrible place: it was sharp with noises, and pains, and hunger, and weakness, and aloneness.

But the Beloved was here. She came when he was almost too exhausted to struggle any more, and they were one again. Her steady pulse flowed through him, and made swooping, restful sounds. And he took her into himself, and was satisfied.

* * *

But then there was the Other.

It rumbled and prodded.

He clung to the Beloved, roaring and fearful, until it went away; but it did not go away for ever. Long, long after, coming up out of the darkness, he found it above him. There were lights set in it that shone down on him, that twinkled. The Other was dark, then pale, then huge and endless.

The Other was odd, strange, amazing. It startled him, made him twitch, made him gape. The Other whispered and it beeped: it bobbed, and it waved.

It was fascinating.

But then he became tired, became empty, and he could feel himself fading. So he called for the Beloved.

But the Other held him prisoner, rocked him, made noises, didn't *understand* that he was in danger.

So he called and called with all his might; and in the end the Beloved came, and gave herself to him to assuage his hunger.

And the Other went away, defeated.

He was the centre of the world, and the Beloved was his servant.

This new world was flat, and pale: it was safe, but not interesting. And so he heaved and heaved and managed to turn his head—and found another new world. He jerked with surprise. There were shapes, and shades, and patterns here.

He called for the Beloved, to make sure she was in this other world, too, and to show her what he had found. But it was the Other who came.

> *Follow your daddy,*
> *My love, my son.*
> *Follow your daddy*
> *Then you'll be a man.*

And so he showed the Other, instead.

2

2

And then people started being unreliable.

It was extremely annoying. *Extremely* annoying: and it wasn't as if he couldn't make his needs known perfectly clearly.

Mummy. Daddy. Truck.

NO!

It did save quite a lot of screaming.

But then things started going wrong.

'Bathtime, Rye.'

Rye had a truck. It tasted salty, like his hands, but it was shinier and colder to lick. Most interesting.

He didn't have time for a bath.

No.

But Mummy didn't understand. She didn't even *try* to understand. She picked Rye up.

Rye hit her with his truck.

No, he told her. *No. NO! NO! NO!*

'Oh yes, my love, or Daddy's supper won't be ready when he gets home. Nice splashy bath!'

How dared she not do as she was told? How *dared* she?

Rye would go under the table where she was too big to follow.

Rye arched his back and almost managed to slip out of her arms, but she only clutched him tighter, so that his vest slipped up roughly against his ribs. She carried him to the bathroom and turned on the taps.

The bathroom was a terrible place to scream. Rye's wails

3

mushroomed and overlapped and magnified themselves until they turned into something like the giants that he almost remembered from when he had first come into this world.

But there was no Beloved to turn to, here. He struggled and fought, but incredibly, incredibly, Mummy, who was always so soft and pretty, fought back; she fought back and he wasn't strong enough.

Rage overtook him. He screamed and screamed, because he had been summoned here and then betrayed by she who had been formed to serve him. He screamed because he was surrounded by giants that were going to eat him up. He fought against the water in the bath, but it got in his mouth and tried to choke him; he fought against his towel, but it smothered him, tangled him, rasped his skin; he fought against his pyjamas, but they bent back his toes.

And then when he tried to break down the bars of his cot they hit him back really hard.

He cried bitterly, then, for Mummy: but she didn't come.

Daddy came, instead. He sat and regarded Rye with bright blue interested eyes.

'I do understand,' he said, after a little while. 'I want to rule the world, too. We'll have to work on it together, eh?'

Rye went to sleep.

3

And then something wonderful happened.

Rye woke up one day in his big new bed to find that something was growling outside: snarly growls, they were, like a bear's.

Rye stood on tiptoe and put his head under the curtain. He could just see something big, like a truck, and bright, bright yellow.

'Yes,' said Mummy. 'It's making a big hole in the road.'

Rye gasped. Making even quite small holes in the flower beds was very naughty. But as for making a great big hole in the *road* . . .

Rye almost burst with respect and envy.

Rye watched and watched the big yellow truck dig the hole. Then he went and hid in a bush until the postman opened the gate.

A nice smelly man discovered him.

'Patting the tracks of the excavator,' he told Mummy. 'Could have been killed.'

'Oh dear lord,' said Mummy, and hugged Rye, and they had to have a drink and some cake to make her feel better.

'Excavator,' said Rye, importantly. '*Excavator*.'

Rye waited until the men were having their tea, next time, and then pushed up the latch of the gate with his spade. He'd got right into the inside of the excavator and pressed all the buttons before he was found.

'Quite a handful, isn't he,' said the smelly man, dourly, and put wire round the latch on the gate.

Mummy made all the excavator men a cake, as a thank-you, and Rye got to lick out the bowl.

Rye got out the next time by climbing onto his tractor, and then onto the dustbins. He managed to get right into the bucket of the excavator, and this time the men were so busy with a big pot of black stinky stuff that they didn't find him for ages.

Rye woke up to find the smelly man scowling at him.

'You know what you're going to get, when you get home,' he said, as he carried Rye back.

'Yes,' said Rye. 'Cake.'

But Daddy opened the door.

That was ever such a surprise, because Daddy didn't usually get home until after Rye had gone to bed.

Daddy took one look at Rye and said, *What's all this?* And Rye suddenly felt as if someone had pushed an icicle into his chest.

And then, instead of having cake and letting Rye out into the garden again to play with his trucks, Daddy walloped him. Rye couldn't believe it at first: he was so surprised he nearly forgot to howl.

And don't let me hear of your being so naughty ever again, Daddy said.

So Rye, who wasn't stupid, made sure that Daddy never heard of his being so naughty ever again.

It took quite a lot of care; but he was a very clever boy, and he managed it.

Daddy began to come home early quite often after that. Daddy was much more interesting, and much cleverer, than Mummy, who quite often wore the wrong clothes, or said the wrong words, or cooked dinner in the wrong way.

They moved to a new house, the biggest in the road.

Dad grew plumper, and his eyes even more twinkly, and his ties became brighter and silkier. Sometimes Dad brought people home to a party, which was great fun, except that sometimes Mum got things wrong. It was strange, because Mum getting things wrong made Dad laugh and laugh when it happened; but then, when all the visitors had gone home, he would be angry and his face would go red and Rye would go away and hide.

Rye hardly ever got things wrong himself, because all you had to do, was to do everything the same as Dad did them.

Dad and Rye went lots of places together. They went to the barber's to get Rye a grown-up haircut, they went to museums, to the docks, to the library, to the zoo, even to work.

There were lots of people at Dad's work. There were guards at the gate, to stop people with bombs, and lots of inside people who all wore white coats and did what Dad said. There was a farm, as well. Dad showed Rye the fattest pig in the world, which was really funny, and Dad explained that by being extra clever he'd managed to make it so that all its piglets would be extra fat, too.

'Would you like to make extra fat pigs when you grow up?' Dad asked, on the way home in the big car.

Rye wanted to drive a dustcart, and squash up all the rubbish; but he wasn't stupid enough to say so. So he said, 'I'd like to *eat* them!'

And that made Dad laugh, and after that they talked about something else.

One day, when Rye was nearly ten, Dad came home, very excited, clutching a fat green bottle of champagne.

'It's come through,' he said. 'I've got the governorship of the new colony.'

The champagne tasted sour, but Dad said it was special, and so Rye sipped it.

Mum looked as if she'd run into a glass wall.

'A new colony? But what about Rye?' she asked, palely.

Dad laughed and dipped his plump lips briefly in the champagne.

'Rye, my dear, will come with us.'

But then Mum spoke back to him. That was something she'd never done before.

'To a new colony? For heaven's sake, Ryland—' But then she stopped abruptly and started again. 'But . . . but . . . children aren't allowed on new colonies, are they?'

Dad laughed again, and his triumph bounced round the living room.

'I'm going to be Governor,' he said. 'Governor, can you understand that, Maria? There'll be a supply ship three times a year, and that's all. I'll be Governor. I'll be in charge. There'll be no one to prevent me from doing anything I please.'

Mum bowed her head, but she was as white as paper.

Rye thought about it. A new colony. A place where Dad was going to be in charge of everything.

It was going to be really marvellous.

Of course it was.

4

The colony would have no roads—and no proper houses, either. They would all have to live in metal boxes, like chickens.

There would be no dustcarts, though there would be tractors and trucks. Rye kept asking about them until in the end Dad got a little impatient.

'There'll be a whole island to tame,' he said. 'We have to make it a marvellous place to live.'

'With excavators?' asked Rye, wistfully.

'Quite possibly. But the new animals and plants and people are much more important and interesting. Remember that.'

Mum worried and worried.

'It'll be a real adventure,' said Dad, grandly. He was getting bouncier by the day. But Mum kept talking to him, very fast, when she thought Rye couldn't hear. But Dad would only say, *Don't be silly, Maria, it's all settled.*

And it was.

Dad went out to the colony first. He sold nearly all the furniture before he went, to save Mum the trouble. Once or twice, when Rye came down for a drink after bedtime, he found Mum flushed and excited and smelling of grown-up trifle. And then she'd talk about explosions and pirates and radiation, and a bitter wind that stripped the skin off you, and beasts with poisonous skin and razor teeth.

But Mum wasn't at all clever; and though she had lived on a colony long ago, and had met Dad there, she was probably getting things muddled.

Rye was much too big for his ride-on excavator, now, so they gave it to a little boy down the road who was really only interested in dinosaurs. When Rye saw it next it was painted green, with big yellow spots and jagged teeth; and he felt sick with guilt.

But there were lots of good things about going to live on the colony.

'I'm not going to go to school any more,' Rye boasted to his friends at playtime, though he quite liked school, really, except for the work, which was dull, and being in trouble, which happened rather a lot. 'I'm going to live on a colony, and Dad's going to be Governor, and I'm going to be the only boy there.'

He was going to be a sort of prince, Rye decided; and he had to run right round the playground twice, just with the excitement of it.

5

The ship was white and constructed in layers, like an ice cream cocktail. Rye strode up and down the first-class walkway and watched the mainland as it receded humbly into the mist.

Rye paced up and down, and climbed about on the first-class brass rails, for days and days, until even the gulls screamed and wheeled and fell away. There was a lifeboat practice, and a pirate practice; but apart from that the ice cream ship wallowed sedately and boringly onward. He wasn't seasick at all.

'Well, you were born on a ship, my love,' said Mum, swallowing bravely. 'So I expect that accounts for it.' Rye had known that story for ages. He had arrived too early, and Dad had had to help him be born himself.

Practically everybody else on the ship was down on the lower-class levels, and to Rye they were only bald spots, or tied-on hats, or sea-thin voices.

'Are there really pirates?' Rye asked the Chief Engineer, when he'd finally persuaded his steward to take him down to the engine room.

'Oh, they're nothing to worry about,' said the Chief Engineer. 'They leave us alone now we've got our new guns.'

Rye was rather disappointed.

'Do they have parrots?' he asked; but the Chief Engineer only laughed, and said they weren't that sort of pirate.

And then, at long last, when Rye had climbed over all the railings on the whole first-class level, even the bits that

11

were quite dangerous, the greyness grew a slightly darker shadow. The waves grew shorter around the ship, jolting her, until she was chugging primly down a narrow channel surrounded by hummocks of silken mud, like a thousand hippos grazing beside the ship.

Everyone crowded round at the front of the ship and chattered and pointed and gazed.

There were dim hills, and now in front there was a low sea wall, and a grey tower that sprouted spindly aerials, and a scatter of metal-box houses that seemed almost as small as the toy trucks that Rye had left back on the mainland with the rest of his life. The wind blew warm, exciting scents at them, full of unknown things.

And then at last, after Mum had finally finished putting on her hat over her sea-curled hair, and even after she'd stopped worrying about tipping the stewards, the gangplank spick-and-spanned the last few feet of mud.

Then there was another frustrating wait. Rye peered down at the third-class deck and kicked the first-class rails.

A line of men in orange uniforms were forming up by the gangway, now: and now they were rumbling down the gangplank. There were other people in uniforms with them: not the white uniforms of the ship's crew, but uniforms more like policemen wore. The men jangled because they were carrying a chain.

No. The chain was fixed to their wrists. To their handcuffs.

Prisoners? thought Rye, astonished. Why had they brought prisoners here?

A marvellous place to live, Dad had said. But—

The prisoners were being led away: yes, up on the hillside there was a long high wire fence and a gatehouse.

But now everybody could leave the ship. People with

12

heavy suitcases were heaving them hurriedly underneath Rye. And there was Dad. There he was, very smart, but not looking this way. Rye pulled Mum along as fast as her little heels would take her.

The gangplank bounced as you walked along it. As Rye placed his first foot on the shore the ship's steady puttering cut out and was swallowed up by the hot damp air.

Rye had arrived on the colony.

And just for a moment he had a strange feeling he was being swallowed by it, too.

6

Dad's tie blazed like a sunrise, and as he shook everyone's hand he was almost dancing with eagerness.

Rye, in the queue to get off the jetty, found himself smiling and smiling and shaking hands with Dad, too.

'Delighted,' said the Governor, as he had said to everyone else; then he laughed, displaying his magnificent extra chin, and ruffled Rye's hair, and then it was Mum's turn to shake hands, and smile tremulously at everyone, and nod the silly Governor's-wife hat that Dad had chosen for her before he'd left the mainland.

Their house was made of metal boxes like all the others, but it was made of more of them. It was quite grand. There was room for a butler (a proper one, a *very* proper one, cigar-shaped and pin-striped); and Teresa, the fierce whirling-dervish of a cook-housekeeper; and a stout young man called Charlie Box, who spent most of his time battling with the slugs in the garden.

There was also a lady called Miss Last, who was so elegantly rigid that everything you said to her turned to blocks of ice in the air and crashed to the floor before it reached her. She was the Governor's secretary, was perfectly efficient in every particular, and somehow made Mum look untidy and uncertain and unhappy.

'And this is Robin Willis,' announced the Governor, jovially. 'My personal assistant, officially; but you'll be doing a certain amount of tutoring, won't you, Willis?'

14

Robin Willis's chunky green jumper was splurging out of the sleeves of his suit and making it too tight under the arms. That was one reason why he was sweating so much; but when Rye looked at him properly he realized that it was mostly because Robin Willis was afraid: his long white face was slack with fear.

And Rye wondered why.

Rye awoke to a comforting, and long-missed, clanking and *hwoof*ing that came to him clearly through the metal walls of the house. Dad worked on his exercise machine every morning, which meant that he was always hugely cheerful at breakfast time, even though other people were feeling as grey and misty as the hills.

'You'll work in your room from nine till four, Rye, generally,' announced the Governor, briskly, patting his mouth with an ice-patterned napkin. 'You'll be able to follow the Prescribed Education Schedules just as if you were at school: Willis will usually be around to give you any help you need. But, for today, you'll be wanting to explore, of course.'

Mum began to flap.

'Go out? By himself?' She was whispering, because she didn't dare speak out loud in front of Havers the butler. 'But . . . Ryland—'

The Governor cleared his throat warningly.

'I expect Rye to survive,' he said, rather in the same way as he might have said, *I expect Rye to do his homework*.

Mum flinched, but she kept twittering on:

'But there might be quicksand,' she said. 'Suck you down before you know it, sand will. And you never know what's lurking out in the hills: vipers, scorpions. And I'm sure I saw some very rough people on the way up here.'

The Governor gave her a look that withered her into a hot-faced muddle.

'We can't all have your exquisite social graces, Maria,' he said, heavily, 'but everyone here is involved in useful work. Just keep away from the prison, Rye, do you hear me? They're settling in a contingent of particularly dangerous prisoners, and the warders will have enough to do as it is.'

Rye's heart bumped with excitement.

'Really? Really dangerous ones? What have they done?'

'That's a secret, I'm afraid, Rye. Now. I'm off to supervise a work party. And I'm sure you'll want to unpack, Maria. Rye!'

Rye stopped getting up.

'Put your napkin tidily, as I have. All right, off you go.'

A marvellous place to live.

At least, it would be, one day. Rye walked down the muddy track and imagined it: a bustling harbour with a fleet of fork-lift trucks buzzing purposefully backwards and forwards, and on the hill a herd of excavators grazing the land, like cows, only a thousand times more elegant and desirable.

But for now things had hardly begun. There was a battered six-ton truck parked outside a warehouse, and that was all, really, apart from two tightly-dressed young women pegging out very small items of clothing on a line. They stopped and stared at him as he approached.

'You must be the Governor's boy,' called the dark one, cheerfully, through bright and shiny lips. 'You're ever so like him.'

People had been saying this to Rye all his life: but there was something about her that made him blush.

'I'm not fat,' he pointed out.

And at that the other girl, the fair fluffy one, flashed her white teeth at him and laughed very loudly.

'He's like a day-old calf, Annie,' she said. 'All skin and too-big bones. He's even got the rumpled poll, look.'

But Annie only gave him a friendly grin, came out through the gate, and took a warm, perfumed hold of his arm.

'Don't mind Noreen,' she said, comfortingly. 'She's always teasing everybody. Now, you're Ryland, aren't you, the same as the Governor? He's told us all about you.'

'Well—I'm called Rye, mostly.'

'Then welcome to the island, Rye. Remember we're here if you need us. And here.'

She took a little cotton bag like one of Mum's lavender bags from her pocket and gave it to him.

He stared at it in surprise.

'It's for luck,' explained Annie. 'Well, for safety, really: sort of like a four-leaf clover—only much stronger, and not actually leafy. Keep it with you, my sweet, especially if you're going up into the hills. All right?'

Rye, very puzzled, and rather hot, crammed the little bag into his pocket.

'There's a good boy,' said Annie; and touched his face for a moment, and went back to the washing line.

As soon as he was out of sight round a bend in the track Rye sat down and tipped the contents of the little bag out onto a rock.

It was hard to be sure, but the bones were probably from some sort of small bird. Yes, that one was the wishbone, like the ones that he and Mum broke between them when Dad wasn't around to be infuriated by Mum's superstitious nonsense. And that twig was scattering little translucent flakes, so—yes, it was actually a small

17

empty-eyed fish. And that dry twisty thing might be—well, it might be anything.

Rye sat and prodded them. He had already noticed that most of the metal-box houses had bunches of stuff hung up outside the door; and the bunch he had looked at closely had proved to contain dead flowers, a shard of very shiny black stone, a crab, a giant earwig hung carefully with a twist of glinting fuse wire round its thorax, and the remains of a bat.

It was all nonsense, of course: this must be supposed to be some sort of magic, and there was no such thing as magic. Dad had said so loads of times.

Though nearly everybody here seemed to believe in it.

It was very strange.

The sky was growing darker, and the hills were marked with slashes of cobalt rain-shadows.

Rye carefully tipped the bits into Annie's bag again, and put the thing back in his pocket.

It was only a ten minute walk from one side of the settlement to the other, and beyond that was only the track that led up towards the prison. There were no proper roads, yet, anywhere, but there was one wide stony track that had had heavy vehicles running along it. Rye wondered what Annie's bag was supposed to protect him *from*. Was Mum right, after all, about the vipers and the quicksand among the ferns and grass?

And then through the warm air there came a voice:
'Sunshine, where are you?
I ain't got no, no no sunshine
Never never, except in my heart.
(That's where I keep it).'

For a moment the sun really seemed to have come out. The voice tossed aside the rain clouds and Rye forgot about vipers and began to stumble as fast as he could up the rough slope towards it.

The place was full of unexpected mounds and hollows. Rye stumbled and tripped his way through the ferns to the top of a slope: and there below him, magnificently, incredibly, was an excavator. A small, but absolutely perfect, excavator. It was such a bright yellow it almost seemed to be singing itself, but it was plainly in trouble. It was leaning sideways so much that the bunch of dried-up things hanging from the cabin roof swung drunkenly, and one of its tracks was almost submerged in sandy mud.

But still someone was singing.

'Sunshine, sweet sunshine!'

Rye slithered down into the dip. His feet got in such a tangle that he nearly slid the last four feet on his backside. He just managed to stop himself: and it was a good thing he did, because lying on the ground at the bottom was a giant.

A singing giant.

'Aargh!' said Rye, coming to a stop by some complicated arrangement of throwing himself backwards and the laws of gravity.

The giant looked round, hit his head on the excavator's grey bumper shielding, winced, and started laughing.

'You made me jump!' he said. 'I saw you coming down and I thought I was going to get myself mugged by one of those big salamanders.'

The giant rolled onto his knees and then neatly to his feet. He held out his hand.

'Gabriel,' he said. 'At your service. And Hercules.'

A man with a brown seamed face popped up jauntily from somewhere and tweaked the peak of his cap. He was quite possibly the weediest man Rye had ever seen.

'And who are you?' asked Gabriel.

Rye had been looking forward to saying 'My father's the Governor' for the last two months; but at the last moment he ducked away from it.

'Rye Makepeace,' he muttered.

The big man grinned.

'Of course you are. Why, you're so much like the Governor I could have picked you out of a thousand. I just hope you've got the Governor's big brain, Rye, because we're stuck halfway down to water-level and we need all the help we can get.'

Rye sighed a little. People were always expecting him to be extra clever, just because Dad was. He turned to look again at the excavator. It was just so marvellously, so neatly, designed, and it looked so undignified and helpless and unbalanced. And it suddenly occurred to Rye that if they dug away the sandy soil behind the submerged tracking . . .

Rye rode home in triumph in the bucket of the excavator, which was called Clarissa.

The most beautiful lady in my life, said Gabriel, proudly.

Mum nearly had a fit. She told Rye he must never, ever, accept lifts from strangers ever again; but the Governor said that no one on the colony was a stranger, and that he was glad Rye was using his brain in a good cause.

'We'll have a game of chess this evening,' he said. 'Good training. You'll enjoy that.'

It turned out they had time for Rye to lose four games in a row before the Governor told him to go to bed.

7

N ine till four.

That was only the same as school; but school had break, lunchtime, assembly, getting things out, tidying up, making people be quiet, punishments, registration, losing things, changing for games, wiping the board, seeing how long it took to make Mr Elkins go purple, packing bags, excuses, fighting for lockers.

Here there was only doing the exercises on the computer and Robin Willis.

Robin Willis—well, Robin Willis was a mess. Everything he wore was violently too small, and his socks never quite matched. He put great gobbets of grease on his hair, presumably to keep shags from nesting in it, so it hung over his narrow forehead like strips of liquorice. Or a depressed squid.

Robin Willis presented Rye's first day's work to him with all the confidence of a man offering a sugar lump to an ivory shark, and tiptoed out backwards. So Rye did it all. Then he put all his books on his shelves, checking all the excavator references in them to make sure they were all still there, down-loaded his CAD system onto his new computer, called up the manufacturer's technical specifications for Clarissa and wondered whether you could incorporate the new hydraulic system from the DA306 model. Then he thought he'd better go across the corridor to the Governor's office to find Robin Willis. The Governor was out: apparently he nearly always was.

'I've finished,' Rye announced; and Robin Willis

21

jumped and floundered, and blinked his daunted eyes.

'So can I go out, now?' asked Rye. 'I mean, you don't want me hanging around, do you? You've got your own work to do for the Governor.'

Robin Willis twitched at the mention of the Governor, and rolled his eyes round rather desperately at the piles of paper all over his desk.

'But . . . the Governor's orders are that you work from nine till four, Rye,' he pointed out, blinking nervously.

That was certainly a problem.

You'll soon zip through the schedules, the Governor had said. *I did the same at your age. Finished the higher biology schedules at fifteen. Aim for that, eh?*

'I could do some Nature Studies while I was out,' Rye suggested. 'Or PE. Dad likes keep-fit. Or Geography.'

A gleam of hope sparked weakly in Robin Willis's pale face.

'Measurement,' he said. 'Er . . . ecology.'

They gazed at each other warily.

'So can I go?' asked Rye, again. He didn't add *Without you telling the Governor?* but the words hung in the air between them.

Robin Willis suddenly dived into the heaps of papers that were zigzagged crazily all over his desk until he found a notebook. He tore out the first page and wrote:

RYLAND MAKEPEACE JUNIOR:
NATURE DIARY

on the cover.

'Take this with you,' he said, with a nervous lick at his lips. 'Er . . . write things in it. But . . . don't let the Governor see you if you can help it. And . . . if the Governor . . . I can't promise—'

22

No, thought Rye, easing the exercise book into his back pocket. Robin Willis was a pathetic quivering wreck who'd hardly say boo to an unhatched gosling, but, whatever he'd been like, he'd hardly have been able to sort out Dad. Rye had been prepared for most things on the colony— for the rain, and the warmth, and the metal-box houses— but he hadn't really been prepared for Dad's being Governor. For Dad's being the Governor all the time, anyway: for his being so absolutely in charge of everything and everyone, always. Dad was still Dad—he was cheerful, enthusiastic, bustling, sharp-eyed, energetic— but when he steamed into view everyone started walking on tiptoes.

It was really a very lucky thing that Dad was so extremely practical and clever.

Clarissa loomed warmly in Rye's imagination as he left the Governor's office, tempting and alluring; but Clarissa and Gabriel would be working down in the settlement. And Dad was down in the settlement. Dad, who was also the Governor.

Rye sighed, checked he'd transferred Annie's bag of magic into his clean trousers, and headed for the beach.

It was hardly a beach, just a metre-wide strip where rubbish had piled up high enough for you to pick your way along without sinking up to your eyebrows in quicksand. Other than that, it was just greasy mounds of mud. Rye tiptoed and balanced and flapped his arms. It was miles better than being stuck inside with the Prescribed Schedules.

The sea wall bent round a little way ahead. That would be the place where everything got washed up. Bits of amber, perhaps, or whales.

Perhaps not whales: the place stank enough of decaying sea-life as it was, without mountains of putrid blubber adding to it: the tinned whale pie they'd had last night

23

had been stomach heaving. Perhaps under the mud there were acres and acres of mud-beans, and all these little crabs that were scuttling about were actually bean-crabs, nibbling at the beans and sending out tiny pongs to haunt the mudflats.

Rye had left the box-houses of the settlement behind, now, and he began to feel as if he was on an adventure. He was going to find something wonderful. A new fish, perhaps, or a massive geode. It'd be so big that he'd have to carry it back on Clarissa, working all the controls himself.

He was so sure there would be something that he looked for it.

And yes. Yes, there. Something quite large and shaggy. Dad had said there were no mammals on the island except for occasional seals and screw-faced bats, but perhaps . . .

Rye looked again and realized what he was looking at.

'Oi!' he said. 'What are you doing here?'

There was a boy squatting by the sea wall; a boy perhaps just a little older than Rye was, with a shock of ill-cut brown hair and narrow grey eyes. The boy looked up at Rye for a second and then got to his feet. He was thin, but neatly built, and just a bit taller than Rye had expected him to be.

'Who are you?' demanded Rye.

'Kris Shoreman,' said the boy, mildly.

Rye was so surprised to see him that he didn't even know whether he was pleased or not.

'But you shouldn't be here,' he pointed out. 'Boys aren't allowed on the colony. I mean, it's all right for me, because Dad's the Governor. But it's too dangerous for just ordinary people.'

The boy Kris nodded.

'Yes,' he said, politely. 'But my ancestors used to live here, you see, so it's all right for me, too.'

24

But of course that couldn't be true.

'They couldn't have done,' said Rye. 'The Governor arrived on the first ship, and that only came a couple of months ago.'

Kris picked up the bucket at his feet. It was half full of bits of smelly fish and crab.

'No one lived here then,' he said, 'but long ago there were people here.'

Rye cast a sharp glance at the boy's narrow eyes and sallow skin.

'Do you mean you're an *offlander*?'

Kris began walking steadily back along the beach, and Rye stumbled along beside him as best he could.

'Dad is. Well, he runs a hot-food stall—that's his job—but Dad's family's offlander. Mum's a warder at the prison.'

Rye almost said, *My mum's a housewife*; but decided against it at the last moment.

'So what are you doing here?'

Kris walked along for a little while without answering; but then offlanders were all a bit slow and stupid like that. That was why they weren't allowed to go to school.

'This place is like a legend to Dad,' he said, at last. 'Aranui's island. That's what offlanders call it: Aranui's island. When Dad found out there was going to be a new colony here he decided we had to come to see it before it was all changed.'

'It's going to be much better, now,' Rye told him. 'Dad—the Governor—he's going to improve everything. Bring lots of people here, and make everything properly organized. The prisoners are going to break stone so we can have proper roads, and Clarissa's going to start clearing the hills so there'll be better farming, and there's going to be a doctor's surgery, and everything.'

Kris nodded, slowly.

'Dad just wanted to know what it was like now,' he said. 'His grandfather was always telling him tales about the ground-shakers, and the healing-pools, and the muse caverns, and the fire-lizards, and the quenchers, and the shark-chanting—'

'The *what*?'

Kris stopped and grinned, suddenly.

'Some of them are offlander things,' he said. 'You know, magic. You wouldn't be interested.'

Rye stood and struggled. Of course he wasn't interested in offlander magic, which was all nonsense.

There was no such thing as magic: Dad had said so.

But what *was* a ground-shaker?

'I could probably show you a fire-lizard,' offered Kris, watching him. 'But it'd be quite a walk.'

Rye thought about it. The fact that everywhere on this island was uphill, through snagging fern and wet grass. And that there might be vipers.

'There's no such thing as a fire-lizard,' Rye said, experimentally. 'Everyone knows that.'

'Well, that's what Dad calls them. But I don't think they are lizards, not really. It's just that they burn if you touch them.'

How could they do that unless they were red hot?

A fire-lizard . . . that sounded like a fairy story. Like a dragon, really.

Or something completely new to science. Rye shivered with sudden excitement.

But then he took a grip on himself. Kris was only an offlander, and everybody knew that offlanders were simple; and people said that they were liars, too. And what did Mum say?

Foolery is catching, that was it.

Rye took a deep, steadying breath.

26

'There's no such thing as a fire-lizard,' he said, again. 'There can't be. You must have got things muddled.'

But then he thought about going back home to Mum's worrying, and Robin Willis's cheese-face, and Teresa's whirling duster that somehow meant that you were always in the way, and he wavered. 'But . . . I'll have a look at them for you if you like,' he said. 'If you can find one.'

And Kris nodded, and vaulted neatly up the sea wall without another word.

8

I t *was* all uphill: Rye stumbled over ant nests and hooked his feet on fern-roots and gasped in the muggy empty air.

'Watch out,' said Kris, mildly, 'those pink fern shoots sting like mad.'

Rye came to a stop, his chest heaving.

'How much further is it?'

'Could be anywhere round here, really . . . if you could manage to breathe a bit more quietly I might be able to hear one.'

Rye did his best. The wind was bustling through the grass, and Clarissa was chugging somewhere a long way away. Apart from that he couldn't hear anything. But Kris nodded again.

'Just over here,' he said, quietly.

Rye ducked under a wild-armed fern and followed Kris up where the rock broke through the earth and fell into an orchid-starred jumble.

'*There*,' said Kris, softly.

It was a moment before Rye saw anything: then two hovering discs of melting gold appeared; and then the thing twitched its tail and he saw it all. Three feet long, with mottled, delicate skin, and a tongue that flicked like a whip.

'Some of the males are twice as big as that,' murmured Kris.

'Wow,' breathed Rye. 'Hey, let's catch it.'

'No. We can't, without a net. They burn if you touch them.'

Rye told himself it wasn't Kris's fault he believed all that stuff.

'They can't do,' Rye said. 'It's only a giant newt or something. How could it?'

Kris hesitated, and then he said: 'I suppose it's magic.'

Rye snorted, but quietly, so as not to frighten the thing off.

'Everybody in this place keeps on about magic,' he said. 'Look what Annie from the hostel gave me.'

Kris pulled open the ribbon and tipped the contents of the bag onto his hand. He viewed everything quietly, and then put it all back again and handed it back to Rye.

'Well?' demanded Rye. '*Is* it magic?'

'Oh yes,' said Kris, tranquilly. 'It was very nice of Annie to think of it. I suppose she knew you wouldn't be getting anything like it from the Governor.'

'Of course not, it's all nonsense . . . what's it supposed to do?'

Kris smiled.

'Well,' he said, 'it keeps away walruses, for one thing.'

That was mad. Totally, totally mad. How could you argue with anything so stupid?

'But . . . there aren't any walruses on the island!' Rye exclaimed, a little exasperated.

'See?' said Kris: and Rye couldn't help but laugh.

'All right,' he said. 'You believe in magic if you like: but I'm still going to catch that beast.'

Rye stepped forward as quietly as he could, going slightly sideways, out of reach of its yellow-lipped mouth.

'No, don't!' said Kris, sharply. 'I told you, it'll take half the skin—'

Rye lunged and grabbed. The salamander's plump body

29

was cool to the touch, and surprisingly heavy. He held it tight, expecting it to lash its tail and wriggle: but instead it went limp.

'Rye!' said Kris. 'Drop it! Let it go or it'll—'

But Rye was discovering for himself that the fire-lizard burned.

Kris shoved Rye's hands in the pool of water that was cupped between the leaf-fronds of the giant fern. As soon as Rye's hands were in it, the burning began to subside. Kris left Rye squatting there and went away to find some pithy water-absorbing leaves that made a dressing good enough to get Rye home. Kris was quite matter-of-fact about it all; he even failed to say *I told you so.*

At home it became clear that the pale goo the fire-lizard had exuded had welded itself to Rye's skin. There were burning blisters all over the palms of his hands.

'Some sort of salamander, by the sound of it,' announced the Governor, briskly, as Mum bathed and anointed and wailed over Rye. 'They'll have to be exterminated, of course. Where did you find them?'

Rye thought about the fire-lizard. About its golden eyes and elegant tail. And Kris had said that some of them were twice as big, twice as old.

He made some vague reply.

9

Kris spent most of his time fishing, or gardening, or helping with the food stall. He wasn't much interested in excavators or engines: in fact he was amazingly ignorant about almost everything, which was frustrating sometimes, especially as he couldn't read or write—but then, as he was an offlander, that wasn't really his fault. Kris was an excellent guide to the island, though. There was one root which, if scraped into a rock pool, would send every fish belly-up between one tide and the next; and another that you could chew endlessly, like gum. And Kris was always picking things, or stowing things away in his backpack; but when Rye asked him what they were, he'd usually just say *magic*.

'There's no such thing,' Rye would say, again and again, with Annie's present stowed safely away in his pocket.

'Take notice of what Kris says, next time, my love,' said Mum, when Havers the butler had shut the front door gently behind Dad, and the whole household had taken its first deep breath for hours.

'But he's just an offlander,' pointed out Rye.

'He may be so, but he's managed to stay alive,' said Mum, with a rare flash of logic.

'Take samples of everything he shows you,' said the Governor, surprisingly broad-minded. 'I'll need full notes, details of habitat. You never know, these primitives may have some useful local knowledge.'

31

The Governor was not the only person who thought so: the Governor was always available to everybody, ready with help, advice, brisk encouragement, and terrifying rage; but people in trouble as often visited the Shoremans' house as the Governor's.

'Kris's dad? You mean Harry Shoreman?' said Gabriel to Rye, who was nearly always welcome to sit in Clarissa's cabin at Gabriel's feet while he worked. 'He's a good guy. Great brain, great crab-burgers.'

'But what about his magic?' asked Rye. 'Isn't he cheating people?'

But Gabriel only laughed, and said he'd never heard anyone making any complaints, and started singing his sunshine song again. And no one did complain: but Rye often found little cairns of stones which proved to have flowers or bits of obsidian or animals inside them, as offerings to the gods.

For life on the colony was hard, especially for the farmers. Every time the supply ship purred sedately up the gleaming channel it brought a dozen new settlers; but each time it took away a dozen others who were wearied by the weather, or by the failure of their crops to flourish in the unremitting damp.

The Governor, always busy, always watchful, and nearly always cheerful, even when his eyes were blazing with huge amounts of anger, had new crops introduced that would cope better with the weather. They grew, slowly and reluctantly, and even proved harvestable; but profits were small, and there was little in the settlement to entertain the men except for another evening's celebration with Annie and the others at the Women's Hostel.

There wasn't a great deal to entertain anyone: Charlie Box spent his time devising ever more ingenious methods of trapping the fat green slugs that devoured the vegetable garden; Miss Last was writing a very secret book about

32

lovey-dovey people in silly clothes; and, when no one was looking, Mum helped Teresa with the housework. If Kris was working, and Gabriel wasn't, then there was nothing much for Rye to do, either, except walk up towards the prison and watch the chain-gangs breaking stones. The prisoners worked with a languid, peaceful rhythm that was quite soothing to watch. Speaking to them was, of course, strictly forbidden; but the warders couldn't be everywhere, and there were a nice couple of old prisoners called Murray and Lott who were always happy to play dice for bits of the jaw-welding toffee that you could get from Mr Reece's store. And once Rye had worked out how they were cheating him, they all became quite good friends.

Rye nearly always spent some time in the evening with the Governor: Rye would lose at chess, or have his schoolwork inspected, or go out to see the Governor's latest project.

It was only occasionally that the Governor was at home in the daytime, luckily, because on those days Rye was stuck in with the Prescribed Schedules. Rye would glower and rumble and pace and fret and design new hydraulic pumps for Clarissa on his CAD system, and look out of the window. If he was lucky he might see the six-ton truck; or the pathetically asthmatic two-stroke tractor that the Governor should in pity have retired to a museum; or Annie, strolling lusciously up to take Gabriel his lunch; or Hercules's mini-dumper. Or, of course, there might be Gabriel himself, singing above the chugging of the gleaming Clarissa. A circle of sunshine seemed to hang over Gabriel's head like an umbrella, and Rye was always very glad to bask in its light.

'Don't you think it would be useful for *me* to be able to work an excavator?' Rye asked Dad, wistfully, one day.

'It'd be much more useful for you to complete your next three science modules,' said the Governor. 'Do that first.'

So Rye did. And then the Governor said, *Well* . . .

Rye knew exactly what to do already. It was a bit confusing co-ordinating the joysticks to start with, and Annie and Gabriel had to run for their lives, shrieking with laughter, on more than one occasion; but when Rye sat on the leather seat, in the wide depression left by Gabriel's backside, he forgot the bundle of dried remains that swung from the cabin roof and felt hollow with wonder and happiness.

10

The colony grew. Squares of fern were burned and scraped away and sown with crops that either struggled to a harvest or rotted in the ground. The Governor brought in ponies to graze on the rough grass; but it proved unsuitable as fodder, and the ponies sulked and kicked and died quite quickly, despite Kris's dogged efforts at doctoring them.

'I'll have Gabriel clear away those rocks for you, Martindale,' said the Governor, who was taking Rye on his tour of all the farmers' smallholdings. 'That'll provide you with another half an acre of productive land.'

But Marty, who had been shocked very nearly sober by the Governor's visit, though he was still astonishingly smelly, looked aghast.

'Aranui's steps?' he asked, the cleaner bits of him paling. '*Move* Aranui's steps? But . . . but that would bring down a curse upon us, for certain, sir!'

'Nonsense,' barked the Governor, hurling a bright blue glance that nearly pushed Marty backwards into his pond, and gave orders for the site to be cleared the next day.

'What *are* Aranui's steps?' asked Rye, on the way home.

'Heaven knows,' said the Governor, petulantly. 'There are quite a few of those arrangements of rock about. I suppose it was an altar or something similar.'

Rye thought about it. About offlander magic, that didn't exist, but that people paid for and didn't complain about.

'Perhaps the steps *should* be left,' he said. 'If they're sort of historical. Especially—'

'*Nonsense!*'

The Governor's sudden rage nearly knocked Rye sideways off the path. 'Don't let me find *you* getting sucked into all that superstitious nonsense!' he snapped. 'It's bad enough with Harry Shoreman playing the witch doctor and frightening people.'

Rye hastily readjusted his ideas: he liked Kris's dad very much—he made brilliant crab-burgers—but it was true that sometimes he seemed to be looking at you from somewhere far, far away. Perhaps he did scare people a bit; and perhaps they did give him presents more often than was strictly speaking necessary.

'Couldn't you stop him doing it?' Rye asked, humbly; but the Governor let out a roar of laughter.

'How? Charge him with witchcraft? That would send Willis into a panic! And Miss Last. You know, I'm almost tempted to do it, just to see their faces.' He walked along, chuckling, all his bad temper evaporated; and Rye was so relieved that he forgot all about Marty and Aranui's steps until the next day, when Clarissa and Gabriel were struck by lightning just as they were lining up to bulldoze the first rock.

They lifted Gabriel up and carried him back to his cabin on a door, where he shivered and moaned, grey-faced, while Annie and Noreen and Dr Naybury took it in turns to feel his forehead and take him meals he couldn't eat. Then, when it was quite clear to the appalled and grief-stricken colony that Gabriel was sinking, Harry Shoreman arrived at Gabriel's house with a bottle of something.

Gabriel sipped it in crab-shellfuls at moonrise and moonfall; and although the smell alone was enough to send Rye retching to the door, Gabriel was on his feet and mourning over Clarissa's burnt-out electrics within a week.

'We're all really glad you're better, Gabriel,' said Rye, poring over a wiring diagram. 'And . . . I'm sure the Governor didn't mean . . . didn't think—'

He found himself unable to find a way out of that sentence; but Gabriel only clapped him on the shoulder and started singing a song about the happiness of being a simple man.

To everyone's relief, the Governor was busy with his next project by the time Rye had worked out how to get Clarissa operational again. The Governor had a hillside sown with a special grass from the mainland. It must have been good stuff, because overnight the place was swarming with the little dun finches that had seemed quite uncommon until then. So the Governor summoned everyone (and that meant everyone) for a week's bird-scaring. And when Marty rolled up one day, very late and squintingly hung-over, the Governor had him tied to a post as a scarecrow while the rest had lunch. It was generally reckoned to be quite a good joke: but no one was late again.

11

There was a whole series of gales the first winter Rye lived on the colony. The Communication Station lost its aerial and the colony was cut off from the mainland for several days. The aerial was put back in the teeth of a warm wild gale that plucked delicate fragments of satin off the Hostel washing lines and left them draped scandalously across the settlement, and Mr Peabody, the Comm Station chief, broke his arm when a swirl of wind swept his ladder right off the tower. Everyone breathed a sigh of relief when the thing was fixed at last. What if there was an emergency? people wondered. What if there was an invasion by these eco-pirates that hated the new colonies so much? What would happen if the colony was cut off from the mainland then?

But they didn't say any of those things to the Governor. He was growing brighter, and more boisterous, every day. Everyone avoided him as much as they could.

'Got to keep things up to scratch!' said the Governor, prancing briskly from one shift-footed colonist to another. 'Don't slouch, Rye. You don't see me slouching, do you?'

Soon after his eleventh birthday, Rye took his Prescribed Education Schedules Three, and, much to Robin Willis's enormous relief and almost cataclysmic sense of gratitude, passed it with magnificently flying colours. Rye was not surprised, but he *was* relieved; his distinction was what the Governor had been expecting.

'That's right,' said the Governor, patting him on the

38

shoulder. 'And, of course, *I* got a distinction at every level, so I shall expect you to keep it up.'

It made Mum happy, too: she had always been thoroughly stupid, and regarded anyone who could do school work with awe: *It must be so nice to be clever*, she said, proudly and absolutely stupidly, as if it had anything at all to do with making you happy. But Rye was glad to see her cheerful: the only other thing that lifted her spirits, apart from a chance to escape to the kitchen to help Teresa, was the thrice-yearly sight of the huddle of failed colonists by the jetty waiting for the supply ship to return them back to the mainland.

'We'll have to give this place up,' she'd say to Rye, with satisfaction, waiting for the delivery of another hundred balls of wool. She kept knitting jumpers for everybody, even though it was hardly ever cold enough to need one. 'No one can live here. This place is cursed, anyone can see that. Another year and we'll be on our way home, you'll see.'

Everybody always gathered to watch as the ship's cargo was winched up and swung out onto the jetty.

Once, there had been juice-fruit.

But the most interesting things the ship unloaded this time were ten pallet-loads of large flat boxes, two dozen uncertain newcomers, and another chain gang of prisoners. These ones wore green armbands over their orange uniforms and marched in step, quite unlike the prisoners' usual reluctant shuffling.

'Eco-pirates,' said Mr Reece, the storekeeper, wisely wagging his beard. 'Saving the planet by blowing up the human population, that's what they're about. Nasty. Hope the Governor's got all his security sorted out.'

The flat boxes didn't look deep enough to contain anything.

'Sliced bread,' suggested young Kevin Frost, brightly.

'Ready-folded loo paper,' said Ned from the Comm Station, with a chuckle. The colony had been making-do with leaves that Kris had collected from something he called a dung bush. Kris had made quite a lot of money.

Now the out-going colonists were making their way up the gangplank. People watched them go with a mixture of contempt and envy.

'Red carpet,' said young Kevin, suddenly. 'That's what's in those boxes. So that His Nibs—'

Ned nudged Kevin violently, and jerked his head at Rye, and everybody else told young Kevin to hold his tongue.

'That's all, for this time,' announced Havers, authoritatively, as the lifting tackle was stowed away back on the ship.

'No it's not, by all the gods,' said Mr Reece, suddenly. 'Look at that!'

More people were coming down the gangplank: no, it was the out-going colonists coming back again. And now the gangplank was being raised and the strip of water between the ship and the jetty was widening. Was too wide.

'What's going on?' asked Ned, uneasily.

Rye found out what was going on that evening when the Governor took him down to the jetty to see the first of the flat boxes being opened.

'Crabs,' said Rye, in astonishment: because if there was one thing the colony wasn't short of, it was crabs. The beach and the mud were full of their drunken scuttling and delicate eating of each other.

The Governor laughed, and his chins bounced with excitement.

'Pentagon crabs, Rye! There's more meat on one of these than ten of the native flat crabs. We'll release them around the estuary, you see, and if we make it illegal to

40

catch them, then in a few years we'll be setting up a canning factory. Magnificent! And all produced to be exactly standard: same size, same colour.'

'Like the pigs,' said Rye. He tried to keep his memories of the mainland alive; he knew he'd left quite a few bits of himself there, and he didn't want to lose them altogether.

The Governor looked at him blankly for a moment, but then he laughed again.

'Certainly, certainly. Remember that, do you? Yes, I knew that would interest you. That sort of thing was an interest of mine when I was your age. Still is, of course.'

'Why didn't the ship take on any passengers?' asked Rye, on the way home.

The Governor rumbled a little.

'The ship's been allotted a new route,' he said at last. 'It goes on to Colony Four, now, to serve the whaling factory there. Much more efficient, but it makes it a longer journey. Makes the ticket a great deal more expensive.'

Rye walked the rest of the way in silence. It was really very clever. Hardly anyone would be able to afford the trip back home, now; and so they would all have to stay on the colony and make the best of things. And so the colony would grow. And now there was no escape, the Governor would be able to make people do anything he wanted.

Now, it wasn't just the men in orange uniforms who were prisoners.

Rye nearly asked if the ship's new route had been the Governor's idea; but then he didn't really need to.

In the night someone went down to the jetty and started crushing the pentagon crabs in their boxes: but luckily the attempt was discovered before much damage was done.

41

Suspicion fell on those who'd been prevented from leaving the colony; but they all turned out to have spent the evening drinking their ticket-money in the Women's Hostel.

So the culprits remained a mystery.

12

Only one person managed to raise enough money to leave the colony: he, unfortunately, was Dr Naybury. Advertisements were placed for another doctor, but they didn't come to anything.

People shook their heads, but the Governor snorted and told everybody they'd better stay healthy, then; and, as no one dared gainsay him, everyone did. They bought obsidian amulets from Harry Shoreman, whose prices were in fact very reasonable; and in the warm moist air the people who had arrived with coughs even began to breathe more easily.

'It'll all be fine,' said Gabriel, whenever people complained. 'The Governor's got more brains than we have: just relax and leave it all to him.'

The new prisoners—the eco-pirates, as Mr Reece had called them—caused no problems, except to the other prisoners, who now, under the new security arrangements, found themselves liable to be searched at any time. Murray was disgusted. 'Blooming pirates,' he complained. 'Flipping boy scouts, more like.'

'But nice boys,' said Lott, trying to be fair. 'Polite.'

Murray snorted.

'They shouldn't be here at all. Just been led astray, that's all. *And* they make a lot of work for Warder Shoreman, them missing their mothers as they do.'

Rye tried to talk to the eco-pirates himself, but they were always doing drill, or polishing their boots, and they were too shy to do more than smile nervously.

'Eco-pirates?' echoed Robin Willis, when Rye asked. 'Well . . . their aim is to protect all living things from extinction or persecution.'

'But there's nothing wrong with that,' said Rye.

'Perhaps not in theory,' said Robin; and wouldn't talk about it any more.

The Governor watched the growing population of the colony with great satisfaction until the last metal house had been bolted together. Then he turned his attention to building. Gabriel cleared half a dozen sites, but there was no clay to make bricks on the island, and no trees, and those that were planted kept going mildewy and wilting away to nothing. The stone that lay under the soggy hills made a firm enough foundation for roads, but it refused to split along regular lines: walls built with it whistled in the wind like kettles coming to the boil. The Governor stayed as active and enthusiastic as ever, but his temper began to lurk, like an ivory shark, very close to the surface. Everyone found themselves liable to attack at all times.

It became very hard for Rye to keep out of trouble.

You got an A Minus?

Clarissa works well enough without your fiddling about with her!

Stand up straight!

Haven't you got anything better to do than loiter about with that Shoreman boy?

Rye found himself keeping as far out of the way as possible, but it wasn't easy. The Governor kept insisting on taking him round to show him everything that was going on.

'You'll find it interesting,' he'd say: and it was pretty well an order.

* * *

44

Rye had been on the island for about two years when there came a day when a rare east wind skirled through the colony, brushing aside the warm westerly and blowing determinedly all night. That was good, because it meant Robin Willis was desperate to scour the beach for seaweed for his collection. To make things even more convenient, the Governor was spending the day inspecting the prison, and it was Harry Shoreman's day for cleaning the burners on the food stall.

'Yes, yes,' said Harry Shoreman, his sleeves rolled up over his intricately tattooed arms. 'I manage. Go. Have good time—not too far, eh, Kris? Weather not good. Aranui cry, maybe.'

'Aranui cry?' asked Rye.

'It might hail,' Kris translated.

Robin Willis was already poking about earnestly on the beach, so Rye and Kris headed up away into the hills. There was a lake about a mile inland where you could catch fish which blew themselves up when you got hold of them, and could be used as water-pistols. Kris loped along easily, and then had to keep waiting for Rye to stumble his way through the ferns.

'I don't know why you don't get tangled up like I do,' Rye complained, tripping and hopping and jarring his back. 'You offlanders are like goats; you must have some built-in root-avoiding device.'

Kris looked at him sidelong.

'It's just something you learn,' he said. 'Like doing your Education Schedules.'

'Anyone can do them.'

'Not quite anyone.'

Rye nearly fell flat on his face over a termite mound.

'You should learn to read,' he said.

Kris shrugged.

'I'm an offlander. Offlanders don't read. Anyway, I'm not allowed to do the exams.'

Rye caught his foot on a jagged bit of rock and nearly tore the sole off his shoe. He wondered if it might be possible to persuade the Governor to build a road out this way. There were now so many prisoners that they were breaking more stones than they could use.

'Look,' said Kris, steadying him. 'See that patch of yellow? That's scratch-pea, that is. It's about the only thing here that flowers all year, even in winter. You can make the petals into a drink, and you can make a curse with the root. Come on.'

The east wind was even stronger up here. It scythed easily through their clothes, and Rye began to feel really cold for the first time since he'd come to the colony.

'Let's go round the other side of the hill,' he said. 'That'll give us a bit of shelter.'

Kris hesitated.

'The bottom's boggy,' he said.

'It'll be all right,' said Rye, wincing away from the wind.

The hail hit them when they were halfway along the valley. There was a swooshing away to the east which grew quickly to a pattering and then to a drum-roll, and then something stung Rye's hand.

'Ow!' he said. 'What the—'

Then a handful of chunks of ice flung themselves at him, and he swung away to protect his face. Beside him, Kris made a squashed squeak of protest. A sudden whisk of wind flipped up Rye's collar and deposited several ice-drippy hailstones down his neck.

Rye pulled his jacket up over his head. Far away the drumming of the hail was swelling to a rumble.

He found himself running, though there was nowhere to run to. Hailstones were crashing down around him. There wasn't time to stop and look, but they must have been the size of finches' eggs.

46

Several crashed into his back, but he was wearing one of Mum's jumpers and they didn't really bother him.

The one that hit the side of his face, did, though. He put his hand up to touch the place and found it sticky.

Kris shouted something over the roar of the crashing stones and turned suddenly to the left. The stones were even larger, now: knobbly things as big and heavy as coins, that clipped his ear and scraped his knuckles.

Now they were down by a place where the hill had long ago fallen away into a rubble of rock. Hailstones ricocheted off the hard surfaces and stung him.

'Rye! This way!'

Kris ducked down and vanished under an overhang of ferns and Rye burrowed in after him.

The darkness of the place amazed him first, and then the silence. He stood and blinked, and breathed, and wiped the trickles of melting ice and blood off on to his sleeves.

'Are you all right?' gasped Kris.

Rye swallowed the salty taste in his mouth.

'What *is* this place?'

'Oh, just a sort of crack in the rock. Did you see the size of those hailstones? I swear one that hit me was as big as an oyster. Nearly had my eye out.'

Rye wasn't listening to Kris. Their breathing was magnified by this place; and, now his eyes were accustomed to the darkness, he could see a glimmer, not towards the outside, but deep and far away.

'What *is* this place?' he said, again, and took a step towards the faint yellow light.

'It's nowhere,' said Kris, hurriedly. 'It doesn't go anywhere special. Listen! I think the hail's turning to rain. We'd better give up on the lake and get back, or my dad will be worried about us. People have been knocked down and died of exposure here before now.'

Rye took a careful step into the darkness. And then another one.

'Don't,' said Kris, urgently. 'Come back. You can't see where you're going. You might fall down a fissure. You might be killed.'

Rye could see a hard edge of crested rock, now, outlined by the faint yellow light beyond. He pushed his feet cautiously across the floor until, much further away than he had thought it was, he touched the rough edge. He side-stepped around it, finding the floor uneven under his feet.

And then he saw.

'Kris,' he whispered, in wonder, and he felt Kris come up behind him. 'Kris, what is it?'

It was a cavern, almost perfectly regular and circular. The walls were spotted with overlapping rounds of lichen, and it was this that seemed to be giving out the light. And over the whole of the walls, snaking round, and over, and through, were the creatures of the colony: snakes and salamanders and finches and gulls and bees and other things Rye didn't recognize, in colours of charcoal and ochre and seashell white.

'It's old,' said Kris, at last, reluctantly. 'It's from the time when there were only offlanders here. It's sort of a secret.'

'What's it for?' asked Rye; but as he asked he knew. It was magic, real magic; the air vibrated with it until it lifted the hairs on the back of his neck.

'It's to keep the island working,' said Kris. 'It's to keep everything woven together so everything can depend on everything else and nothing fails.'

'That's rubbish,' said Rye, as robustly as he could. 'That way everything just stays the same.'

There was a pause, and then Kris said, mildly: 'It's just offlander stuff. And it is very old.'

There was a pointed arch of darkness across on the other side of the chamber.

'What's through there?'

'Nothing,' said Kris, uneasily. 'Nothing much.'

It was a pool. It was still and tranquil, except for when a drop of water fell from the end of one of the great band of pillars that hung from the invisible roof. Then there was a sound like a note on a glockenspiel, so that it raced straight to your heart.

'Look!' said Rye; but in his excitement he spoke too loudly, and mashed the stillness of the place with echoes. 'What are they?'

Kris knelt down by the pool quietly, neatly, almost as if he was doing homage to something. Then he gently scooped up a handful of water and held it out for Rye to see.

The creature was almost transparent; almost as if the water of the pool had solidified into life. Rye put out a finger to poke it, and then didn't quite want to.

'It's a quencher,' whispered Kris. 'A salamander, I suppose you'd call it, but it's not the same as the outside sort you get on the hills. These live in the caves all their lives. See, they don't have any eyes?'

Rye peered closely. This place was spooking him even more than the painted chamber had, sending shivers down his spine. So he said, roughly:

'What's the use of a thing like that?'

Kris lowered his hands gently into the water and let the quencher swim away.

'They cool Aranui's fever.'

'*What?*'

'They keep him quiet, so he does not toss and turn and cause the earth to tremble and break its skin.'

Rye frowned and tried to disentangle some meaning from all the nonsense.

'You mean they stop earthquakes? That's crazy. That's really crazy. You can't believe that.'

Kris shrugged, and went on in a quiet voice that sounded as if he were reciting poetry.

'This is the centre of the earth. It is the foundation upon which the hills sit.' Then he broke off and frowned. 'It sounds odd in your language.'

'It'd sound crazy in any language,' said Rye, suddenly reassured. He scrambled to his feet. 'How far do the caves go?'

'I don't know. I don't think anyone does. The lichen doesn't grow much after this cavern, so you can't see. And there really are fissures in the floor big enough to fall down. Anyway, there's been a rock-fall, so you can't go much further any more, but Dad says there are tales of a whole system reaching back to the sea.'

Sure enough, once you were past the pool cavern the lichen failed and Rye found himself in a draughty blackness that smelt faintly of stagnant water.

He waved his hand in front of his face and to his wonder saw absolutely nothing.

He grunted, and turned back.

The sun was shining when they came out of the caves.

'We'd better get back,' said Kris. 'Dad'll be worried.'

'All right. It's too cold to swim, anyway.'

'Rye!'

'What?'

'It *is* a secret. A really really important one.'

'It's all just nonsense,' said Rye, brushing away his memories of the way his hair had stood on end.

Kris looked at him searchingly.

'Yes,' he said. 'Just offlander nonsense. Not worth bothering with.'

'That's right,' said Rye.

A little further along they heard shouts and spotted little brown figures hurrying over the hills towards them.

They were looking for Rye.

13

K ris melted away immediately. It was all you could have expected of him; and in any case, there was nothing he could have done to help. The Governor had discovered that Rye was out on the hills in the hailstorm when he should have been at his lessons.

Things might not have been so bad if one of the search party hadn't spotted a pale something sprawled by the sea-wall. Robin Willis was unconscious and battered, but he began to come round as soon as they lifted him up; which meant that, of course, he was at the most pathetic possible stage of groaning and flopping about when they carried him into the house.

Mum made the most of their wounds. She bathed Rye's face (he'd forgotten all about the cut from the hailstone, but apparently it had bled quite spectacularly), and she brought in quantities of warm blankets to wrap them in. Robin Willis, of course, was properly hurt: he couldn't remember what had happened, but presumably he'd slipped and had been careless enough to crack his head. The blow had turned him an unpleasant shade of violet, and he wasn't able to drink the hot tea Mum kept pressing on them. So Mum wiped his face and towelled his hair until it stood on end and made him look like a very lost baboon.

'How did Dad find out?' asked Rye, abruptly, hunched under his blankets. He'd been expecting the Governor to be at home, fuming, but there was no sign of him, except in everyone's listening faces.

Mum put a bowl of hot water on the floor in front of Rye and began undoing his shoelaces.

'You were seen setting off by one of the warders,' she said. 'And when the hail started he thought he'd better let Dad know. Oh, and I've been so worried, Rye: I thought you were in your room, working. Oh, how can anyone live here?'

Rye's sense of doom increased.

'There,' said Mum. 'I've had some mustard put in the bowl. In they go.'

Rye lowered his feet cautiously into the hot water.

'He won't be back until six o'clock,' said Mum, in some attempt at comfort.

Time passed very slowly.

Robin Willis, of course, had taken a chill. By six o'clock he was trembling and cream-faced and hardly able to stutter through his chattering teeth. Rye, shivering in his own room, wondered if he might be going to be ill himself; but that was just wishful thinking.

If Robin Willis had been well they could probably have woven together some story to appease the Governor to some extent: something to do with meteorology, perhaps. Rye had concocted several stories that would certainly have helped, and one which might possibly even have done the whole job. But Robin Willis was too ill to be able to talk much at all: and in any case, expecting him to stand up to the Governor would have been like expecting an earwig to stand up to Clarissa.

The whole house seemed to be waiting for the Governor: it became so still, so sensitive, that it flinched when he opened the gate, as if his wrath had preceded him like the bow-wave on a ship. And when the Governor stepped onto the doormat the whole house went instantly to scorching point. The servants tiptoed to the furthest parts of the house; even Miss Last deserted her frustrated lovers and took her elegantly stockinged legs out of the back door for a walk.

The Governor summoned Robin Willis and Rye. He stood, with his feet apart and his eyes piercing right into the centre of Rye's soul, and rapped out precisely all the questions Rye had hoped he would not think to ask, one after the other. And Robin Willis stuttered and spluttered and gasped pallidly and failed to avoid answering any of them.

Mum was brave, but worse than useless: she stood in the doorway and chirruped. There was nothing Rye could do, so he kept quiet and still and did nothing. He was practically certain the Governor was going to hit him; though he didn't know why he was so sure, because as far as he could remember the Governor had never hit him before, had never even threatened him. But Rye had always, always, always known it might happen. He had always been afraid: it was odd, because he'd never realized that before. He'd always been careful to do as the Governor said, to do as the Governor did, but he'd always assumed it was more or less because the Governor was especially clever and especially important: but mostly it had been because Rye had been afraid, just as Robin Willis and Mum were afraid.

The Governor didn't waste time. He demolished any excuses Robin Willis might have offered, and dismissed him shivering back to his room.

Mum was chirruping again; but it would have been better if she'd held her tongue.

'The important thing is that Rye's safe,' she twittered.

'Safe?' snapped the Governor, and let out a hoarse bray. 'When he's been off in the hills when he should have been at his work? That's the last thing he is.' And then his searchlight eyes swivelled above his heavy jowls. They focused their beam deep, deep inside Rye.

Rye felt a new dismay sweeping over him.

'You're hardly battered about at all,' the Governor said. 'You're not half as bashed about as poor Willis is. You must have found shelter, I suppose. Shelter, up in the hills. That's interesting. Where?'

Rye felt himself go hot, then cold.

'There was a . . . an overhang of rock,' he blurted out.

But it was no use: no use at all.

The Governor kept his eyes on Rye and went terribly still.

'Tell me where you sheltered,' he said quietly; and all Rye's bones clenched themselves together.

It was a secret, Kris had said.

But it was only an *offlander* secret.

Rye ought to tell: the Governor must always know what was going on.

It wouldn't matter, anyway.

And he hadn't made any promises.

But . . . but it was a secret.

Kris had said so.

A silly offlander magic secret.

But if he didn't tell—

'Well?'

Somehow, almost without Rye's having anything to do with it, someone said, *There was a cave.*

That was all that happened. He didn't say anything about Kris, or the painted cavern, or the magic that had stood his hair on end, or the quenchers. He even said he didn't know where the entrance was, which wasn't completely the truth.

But the Governor's rage suddenly vanished. Evaporated.

Caves, he said, suddenly beaming. *If there are caves then we could perhaps transfer the prisoners underground. Use the prison buildings to house more colonists. Excellent!*

55

And the Governor rubbed his hands together and rang the bell and gave orders for dynamite and lamps and pneumatic drills.

When that was done, he took Rye into his office.

And when he had finished that business, he went out again to supervise his men.

14

The Governor inspected Rye's day's work, as he had promised.

'Good,' he said, flicking through it with his thumbnail and handing it back. 'That's more what I expect, Rye. You won't get anywhere without application. When I was your age I was three years ahead of the Schedules, and all by private study.'

And Rye wanted to hit him.

That evening, as usual, the Governor took Rye out. The way into the cave system had been easy to find, once there'd been the clue that it was there; all they'd had to do was dynamite the place where the river poured out of the rock.

They'd found their way to a series of three big caverns already. The Governor was delighted.

'And there will be more,' he said. 'There's been a rock-fall here, you see, so we're held up for the moment; but we'll bring blasting-gear in tomorrow and see what we'll see. Be prepared for a few big bangs then, eh?'

Thousands of years of rain had deposited huge veins and columns down the walls of the caves. It was like a temple, thought Rye, standing in the very centre and trying to catch a trace of the magic he'd felt the day before.

But the Governor was still talking.

'We'll have to blast away this section of rock,' he said happily. 'And divert the river, obviously: that'll be a big job, but we don't want people falling in, ha!'

The Governor bustled over to him.

'Come and see, come and see,' he said. 'Look, the rock forms a sort of alcove here. We'll be able to drive bars into the rock and use it as a holding area. Might have been made on purpose!'

The alcove was stained with cream and rust-coloured streaks. They swayed and tangled round each other and reminded Rye of the animals' cavern over a mile away on the other side of the hill.

He suddenly turned to the Governor.

'It's not right,' he said.

'What? What? What's not right?'

Rye was not nearly as afraid as he should have been. He didn't understand it.

'Using these caves,' he said. 'Spoiling them.'

The Governor's eyes flashed, but Rye still was not really afraid. It was very odd.

'So, are you sorry for the poor prisoners, or do you want to preserve the caves for tourism?'

That was horrible, because those two things were exactly what was in Rye's mind: the dreadfulness of being underground for years on end; and the contradictory picture of crowds of people, stepping softly, uplifted and in awe, through the endless caverns.

'You mustn't do it,' he said, though he knew it was stupid. There was no point in talking about offlander magic, but he went on, doggedly. 'These caves—they don't belong to us.'

The Governor was watching him intently; not angry at all, but curious, fascinated.

'To whom do they belong?' he asked.

Rye tried to work it out.

'To themselves,' he said, though that was stupid, too. 'To the colony. To the island.'

The Governor laughed softly.

'And to whom does the island belong?'

Rye stood there, stubbornly, but he couldn't grasp the answer that he knew was there.

The Governor put a hand on Rye's shoulder.

'The colony's mine, Rye. You know that. It's mine, to do with as I like.'

'It's not,' said Rye; but without hope.

'Oh, yes. Oh yes. And do you know what I'm going to do, Rye? I am going to make it a shining example of human activity and happiness.' He looked round, and nodded. 'It'll take time. But I'll get there in the end.'

They walked together back through the caves and out into the open. The mudflats lay before them, humped and almost endless, smelling of salt and decay.

'It won't work,' said Rye. 'You've got it all wrong.'

Their blue eyes caught and held each other.

'You're very stubborn, Rye,' said the Governor, gently. 'But then so am I.'

'No,' said Rye, glaring. 'I'm not like you at all.'

The Governor laughed.

'Stubborn, and clever, and dark, and wilful,' he mused.

They turned the corner and saw the colony spread out before them, the little lights in the houses winking through the dusk.

The Governor paused to admire it.

'There it is, Rye,' he said. 'Your legacy. Think of that.'

And Rye realized that he was yet another person who did not possess his boat fare home.

15

The Governor was late home on the fourth day after that.

'I'm going out,' Rye told Mum. He'd been working inside all day and had designed a new and much more elegant way of transferring Clarissa from steel to rubber tracking (not that she ever needed rubber tracking, here) and he was now three more weeks ahead of the blasted Schedules.

'Out? Oh, but, Rye, my love, the weather doesn't look very nice.'

'It never does.'

'Well,' said Mum, with mollusc-like tenacity, 'just don't go far. And don't be late.'

'All right, all right.'

Mum followed him right out to the hall.

'I'm not sure Dad would want you to go out after what happened the other day,' she said. 'So *don't* be late.' There was a pleading note to her voice that annoyed him.

It was an incredible relief to be alone. Rye breathed deep of the warm moist air and felt immeasurably lighter.

He followed the sound of Clarissa's exquisitely tuned engines and Gabriel's lusty song almost up to the cave entrance.

'You're working late,' he called to Gabriel.

Gabriel beamed like a sunny day and lifted a huge hand in acknowledgement.

'Got to get the road finished before the heavy machinery comes in, Rye.'

'Can I help?'

But Gabriel shook his head.

'Sorry, but the Governor needs me to get all the way to that marker before dark, and I'm only just going to make it as it is.'

The marker was a whitewashed stone, glowing in the half-light.

'I could move it this way a bit,' offered Rye; and Gabriel grinned, but shook his head.

'Thanks,' he said. 'But I guess it'll be best if I follow orders, Rye, just the same as everybody else.'

And Rye went away feeling as if he'd been told off.

Kris was up on the hillside cutting the coarse unkillable fern that flourished there. It burned well, if only you could get it properly dry.

'Kris!' called Rye, from the path.

Kris paused for a moment, as if he'd heard; but then he carried on deftly skimming his knife across the stems.

Rye ploughed up to him through the wet grass.

'Do you want any help?' he asked. 'I'll bundle up the fern for you if you like.'

Kris shot him a cold sideways glance through his narrow eyes.

'No thank you,' he said, shortly; and bent back to his work.

Rye wavered, unsure whether to go or stay.

Kris's hooked knife was so sharp it hardly moved the stalks: they toppled and bounced gracefully on the ground and then Kris gathered up the cut pieces and shoved them down together hard.

Rye began to feel uneasy. He might as well go back down to the settlement if Kris was in a funny mood: Kris was an offlander, after all, and you never could work out just how their minds worked.

Kris was an offlander, just as the caves that the Governor was destroying were offlander caves.

Rye remembered the twining animals. And the magic, the real magic, that had lifted the hairs on his neck.

Suddenly it was as if Rye was looking at everything from a different place.

'I'm sorry my dad found out about the caves,' he said suddenly.

But Kris didn't answer. For two years, whatever Rye had said about offlanders, about magic, about the gods, Kris had never been angry. But Kris was angry now.

Rye shivered, and felt suddenly empty.

Look at me, he wanted to say.

But there was only one way he could think of to make Kris look at him.

Kris's knife cut through three more stalks with a *snick-snick-snick*.

And Rye took the plunge.

'But you offlanders can't expect to keep the caves to yourselves,' he said. 'That would be selfish. A waste. But of course I can't expect you to understand that. I mean, you've not had any education, you're practically savages. You're so primitive you actually still believe in magic. You're just not used to the idea of logical thought.'

Kris bent down to stack a new bundle of fern. He did it neatly, methodically, but he was suddenly breathing fast.

Rye did what he could to get himself ready, and carried on talking.

'You wait until you see how much the caves are improved,' he went on; and as he talked, he listened to himself, and was appalled that these had ever been his sort of thoughts. 'You needn't worry about all the destruction,' he went on. 'Everything will be recorded scientifically. Those salamanders, for example—what was your funny name for them? Wrenchers?—I'm sure they'll be properly investigated. Preserved, I expect. In formaldehyde or something.'

Kris had gone white, but his knife was still singing neatly through the air to slash the fern dead.

How much more will it take? thought Rye, and his heart began to pound. But he didn't stop.

'I mean, it must be difficult when your father's only an offlander,' he went on. 'It means you've been sort of sucking in all his nonsense since you were born. Not that your father can *help* being like that—you know, so ignorant and stupid—though I wish he'd get rid of all those silly tattoos—it's just—'

Rye was too slow, much too slow. He'd thought he'd been ready, but Kris had swung round and struck out before he could move. Kris's knuckles hit the bones of Rye's eye socket with an appalling knock.

Rye went over like a skittle, hit the ground, and rolled. Then the bit of his mind that wasn't occupied with how much his face hurt saw something falling down on top of him, so he put up his arm to protect his head.

And then he was going downhill—not really rolling, but jolting and jerking and jarring, while the bruised sky and the dark earth jolted round him. He kicked out to try to stop himself, but everything was going too fast to work out how to do it. He managed to clutch hold of something, but it whipped itself away, scorching his palm. And now something big was coming down with him, round and round. It kept hitting out at him, but not very hard, because everything was so dizzy and confused.

The first Rye knew about the bottom of the slope was when he fell a clear vertical foot and hit a sheet of cold water. By the time he'd opened his mouth to yell he was sinking into an infinite wallow of mud. Thick, oozing mud.

He paddled and kicked frantically, tipped backwards, tried again more purposefully, found the bottom, and managed to push himself to his feet. The muddy water only came up to his ribs, but he was covered, slicked down, saturated, with dark green stinking slime. He stood and puffed and snorted and gasped and sneezed and dripped and stank.

After quite a while he pushed aside the glutinous strips of hair that were dripping noisome sludge into his mouth, wiped his forehead with a slimy sleeve, and ventured to open his eyes.

Kris was watching him from a couple of feet above the edge of the pond, and Rye had never seen anyone look so utterly peaceful and completely fulfilled. Rye wiped his mouth, blew a disgusted raspberry to expel some more of the mud, and managed to find his voice.

'Do you feel better now?' he said.

Kris grinned blissfully.

'Yes. I do, as a matter of fact.'

'Help me out, then.'

There was another pool just a little way away. Rye managed to scoop up enough water off the top to sluice himself down. He found a frog down his vest.

'I think my face is swelling,' he said, touching his cheekbone with tender fingers.

Kris looked at him critically.

'It's going to be blown up like a bullfrog's in another half an hour,' he said, with interest, and a little pride.

'Brilliant. Heaven knows what I'm going to tell my dad.'

At the mention of the Governor the air between them grew cold again. So Rye said:

'I didn't mean to tell the Governor about the caves.

Honestly, Kris. But he worked out I'd sheltered somewhere. And he can always get into my mind, somehow. I didn't tell him where the entrance was, or anything about them.'

And Kris sighed.

'I should never have shown you,' he said. 'It was stupid, giving away secrets like that. Even if they were only about ignorant non-existent offlander magics.'

Rye sighed, then.

'I didn't mean any of that, either,' he said. 'I just thought you'd feel better if you hit someone.'

'I know,' said Kris.

Mum tried to hide the swelling on Rye's face with make-up, and then, when that didn't work, she tried twittering on about mumps. And bee stings.

None of it fooled the Governor for a second.

'Was it a good fight?' he asked, with interest.

'Not really,' said Rye, sadly.

'Well, I hope you gave as good as you got.'

It had all been a jumble; Rye couldn't have sworn to hitting Kris at all. He hadn't really been trying to.

'No. I lost.'

The Governor sat and ruminated for a little while.

'You're not in the easiest situation,' he said at last. 'People will be jealous—resent your position. Is there anything you'd like me to sort out?'

Rye thought about Kris, and the Governor's sortings-out.

He said *'No thank you,'* and went to bed.

16

The next ship brought in a lot of mining machinery, and a battery-powered truck that pulled a trio of spoil-trolleys. Rye tried to be enthusiastic about them, but they were rusty and battered and they had none of Clarissa's elegance.

'Well,' said Mum, when he complained. 'I expect Dad spent most of his budget on Clarissa for you.'

The colony became a confusion of roaring and bangs and changing gears until you could hardly detect the keening of the gulls or the greater silence of the hills. The caves were enlarged, and redesigned; the cave system was so extensive that the Governor gave up exploring and sealed off the tunnels with metal grilles. Clarissa stood deserted for days while Gabriel helped the trolley-men: and sometimes if you walked on the hill you could hear his singing coming up faintly through the earth beneath you.

The hills were tunnelled into busily and slowly until at last the drill-men came across a wide stratum of rock, as pale and crumbly as cheese, which was so soft that the water cooling the drills was almost enough to shift it by itself. Everything was suddenly much easier. The river, with much drilling and dynamiting and very nearly a drowning, was provided with a new channel; and the salamander pool and the painted cave remained undiscovered and undefiled.

The eco-pirates, disciplined and impenetrable, showed no sign of caring about the move to the new cave-prison one way or the other; but the other prisoners were inclined to sulk. Lotty grumbled about rheumatism, and Murray, who was engaged in an exquisite depiction of his life-history in embroidery silk, kept complaining about the inadequacy of artificial light. The only reason for discontent among the colonists was that all the machinery had left less room than usual on the ship for other cargo: and so luxuries—coffee, chocolate, paper, shampoo—were in short supply.

Under these circumstances a spirit of self-help began to develop among the colonists, and Mr Peabody and Ned from the Comm Station looked out old paraffin containers in which to brew fern beer.

But they had reckoned without Mrs Hook, the formidable proprietress of the Women's Hostel, who had no desire for such competition. She declared that home brewing should be made illegal, and marched on the Governor's residence.

It was the nearest thing to a heavyweight fight the colony had seen, and everyone waited breathlessly for the roof to explode off the Governor's house; but in fact the Governor was charming, told Mrs Hook she was an indispensable asset to the colony, and sent her home, unsuccessful but rather gratified. His health was drunk with awe in metal-box houses across the colony for a month afterwards.

Rye sat glumly at home. He upgraded his CAD system, did quite a lot of research into rust-prevention, and trudged through the Schedules until after three weeks he could feel his brain cells committing suicide with boredom. He even found himself looking out for Annie in the hope of inveigling her into a through-the-window chat; and that was so pathetic that Rye did a huge history project on Leisure Through the Ages, coloured everything in really nicely, and showed it to the Governor.

'Now,' said Rye, turning to page four. 'Look at all the holidays we'd have if we were Thanian. Seventy-six days a year, that comes to. On the other hand, according to the creation myth of the Riath Indians, I should be getting four days off in every eight-day week.'

'Very interesting,' said the Governor, peering at the key.

'Isn't it? Now, look at this: the Culobi Tribe believes it brings bad luck to work at full moon. There are quite a lot of beliefs centred on the moon. They're all on this page here. And over here you can see that in Ditaan the people are forbidden by law to work on the weekday they were born on.'

The Governor turned the pages, and cross-checked things; and in the end he laughed, and talked to Robin Willis, and Rye ended up with two days off a week, and two o'clock finish if his work was done and Robin Willis was available to check it, and even a whole week's holiday whenever the ship came.

So Rye had quite a lot of time on his hands. He would generally go and pay his respects to Clarissa and Gabriel and have a really serious discussion about armrest-situated control panels, or turning radii; or perhaps he'd help with coaxing the ancient tractor into life. Then he'd generally go and find Kris, which quite often meant helping with the food stall. Luckily the Governor was very busy at the caves, so he only made occasional comments about Rye frittering away his time.

'Crab-frittering away your time,' said Kris, expertly flipping burgers.

'He wants me to be Governor, one day,' said Rye.

'And . . . don't you want to?'

'I don't think it matters much what I want.'

Or sometimes Rye would go up to the prison, to have a chat to Murray and Lotty, or watch the Pirates v. the Lags at

68

football. Or he'd go to the Comm Station, to see if Ned had time to do some of his conjuring tricks. Or, if Lisa was off-duty, he'd go up to the Shoremans' house. Kris's mum was big, and fair, and never sad; and she was pleased to have someone to help her poke gentle fun at offlander ways.

Rye was surprised by how disappointed he was to find Harry so seldom at home.

'Dad's got a lot to do,' said Kris, soberly. 'He's worried about the work the Governor's doing underground.'

'They haven't found your offlander caves,' said Rye. 'They're all safely gridded off, now.'

'Yes, I know. But what other magics have they disturbed, Rye, down inside the hills?'

Rye thought about the magic he'd felt inside the caves, and he thought about the lightning that had struck Gabriel. The contents of Annie's little cloth bag had long ago disintegrated into dust, but he still carried it with him.

'You don't think . . . you don't think something's going to happen, do you?' he asked.

'Dad's working really hard,' said Kris. 'He's working with a thousand years of magic. Generations of wisdom and lore.'

Yes, Rye found he could believe that. Sometimes, when you met him on the hills, you could feel Harry's magic: it hung about him like a cloak of power.

Rye relaxed a little.

'So it'll be all right,' he said.

Kris looked at him; and then he laughed a little, weakly.

'It's going to be like throwing a cough-sweet at a tidal-wave,' he said.

'Could you teach *me* some magic?' asked Rye, one day, when Harry was home for once. Kris would never tell him anything.

Harry grinned, and let out a stream of words that rippled through the air like hot tar.

Kris grinned, too, at the expression on Rye's face.

'I'll teach it to you in your language,' he said.

> *Aranui, Aranui,*
> *Netter of souls,*
> *Cast your eyes*
> *To the horizon*
> *And let your mighty feet*
> *Pass us by.*

> *Aranui, Aranui,*
> *Destroyer of islands,*
> *Fold your hands.*
> *For we are too small*
> *For your glory*
> *Or service.*

And Rye learned it carefully, and often said it to himself to keep it fresh in his mind. For it felt powerful.

'So why *did* you marry an offlander?' Rye asked Lisa one day, when Harry had been boiling up some particularly noisome ingredients, and Harry and Kris had been singing part of the shark-chant, that lured the ivory sharks into the bay to be slaughtered.

Harry Shoreman gave a shout of mock despair.

'Moustaches!' he exclaimed. 'I very handsome man. Big moustaches, slim, good muscles, very sexy. Just like now, huh? And Lisa, see, she bigger than me. Fast runner. I, no chance. Caught. Finished. No. Worse than that! *Married.*'

And then Lisa caught up her warder's baton and chased him round the house, Kris tied himself in knots with embarrassment and revulsion, and Rye laughed so much that the string of the offlander net he was making got tangled and he had to spend ages unpicking things.

As he did, he found himself wondering about his own parents. They were at least as odd a mixture as Kris's own. Mum and Dad had met on another new colony, he knew that; but why on earth had Dad gone and saddled himself with Mum?

But it wasn't very nice to think about, so he banished it from his mind.

The next supply ship brought another chain gang of green armbanded eco-pirates to join the prisoners recently installed in the caves. Rye and Kris went as close as they were allowed and watched them marching smartly down the gangplank and off up the road. The new cave-prison and the area around and over it was now strictly out of bounds to everyone except prison staff. Gabriel wouldn't even give Rye a lift up there.

'But why not?' said Rye, aggrieved. 'I couldn't do anything if I was with you, Gabriel.'

'Governor's orders, Rye.'

'But he wouldn't know!'

That made Gabriel laugh for a long time. But he only said, 'It's not my place to argue with the Governor, Rye. And I sing thanks to the gods every day for that.'

And that *was* that.

'I wonder exactly what they've done,' said Rye to Kris, as the prisoners marched past. This column was led by a thin, beaky-nosed man with an extra high forehead, but from where Rye stood the rest looked just ordinary. 'I mean, I know it's all to do with saving the world, but I wonder what they've done to be put in prison?'

Kris didn't answer for a while. Then he said, 'I wonder why none of them ever gets released.'

Now Kris came to mention it, Rye wondered about that, too.

The ship unloaded large numbers of barrels and nets and pallets onto the jetty. Then it sounded its foghorn and put its engines into reverse.

It wasn't until the last pallet-load of flour bags had been scooped up by the fork-lift truck and taken away to the safety of the warehouse that anyone realized there was something still left on the concrete.

It was a girl.

17

Everybody in the colony saw the girl—except perhaps the Governor, who was very busy talking to Mr Franklyn the prison manager. At any rate, the Governor bustled off, his silk tie shining before him in a fanfare of clashing colours, without his seeming to realize she was there.

But that was incredible: the Governor noticed everything.

Rye and Kris exchanged glances. The girl was probably about their age. She had a white bony forehead and white bony legs and scraped-back frizzy hair. She had no luggage.

The colonists shuffled their feet and wondered.

There was only one other person on the jetty, now: a soft, honey-haired woman in lumpy clothes whose job it had been to smile at the newcomers after the Governor had wrung their hands.

Everybody waited for the Governor's wife to walk away and leave the girl, too. But instead she walked up to her, spoke briefly, and then began to lead her up the road towards the Governor's house.

When Rye got home, the girl was sitting, very straight, on one of the chairs in the hall. Her face was as closed off as a brick wall.

Rye pursued Mum, but voices halted him before he found her.

He could hear everything quite clearly, even without putting his ear to the door. The Governor's voice was big and rumbly and tended to travel along the metal walls to every corner of the house at the best of times. And the person with him was worried and upset.

'But she says she's got nowhere to go,' said Mum, faint and fluttery.

'I'm afraid that's quite true, Maria. She shouldn't be on the island at all, really. She's only been sent here because no one knows what else to do with her.'

'Oh . . . but . . . but *you* can sort it all out, Ryland. You're Governor. You can sort anything out.'

The Governor laughed—not his usual triumphant bray, but something softer, almost surprised-sounding. 'My dear,' he said, 'the best thing I can do for Stefanie Arne is not to know she's here.'

There was a pause, and Rye got ready to hide in case Mum came out in a flap. But instead she said, bewildered, but dogged, 'But she's got nowhere to go!'

And still the Governor didn't snap her quiet.

'I know, my dear, I know,' he said. 'So—we need somewhere to put her, then. Somewhere where she can't cause trouble. You could help her, Maria, couldn't you. With clothes and so on.'

'But where, Ryland? There's no one who would want to care for her, is there, except me?'

There was quite a long pause. And then the Governor said, quietly, 'She'll have to stay at the Hostel, then. Arrange it, Maria, will you? We can find some money, I suppose, for them to look after the girl. Tell Mrs Hook her licence depends on them keeping her safe. Well. Fed.'

And a longer pause. And then someone was approaching the door. Rye hastened backwards and managed to get behind the door of the cloakroom.

He heard one more thing.

'It's been foolish of me to have such faith in you, Ryland,' said Mum.

18

'R ye!'

Rye tried to look as if there was a perfectly natural reason for his being in the cloakroom.

'I need some of your clothes, my love,' said Mum, her hand on his bedroom door.

'My *what*?'

'For Stefanie.'

Rye was so thrown off balance he found himself rumbling and grumbling almost at random.

'They'll be too big,' he objected. 'And they're boys' clothes.'

'I know, but they'll have to do until I can alter some things for her. Is there anything you're especially fond of?'

'Well—'

Rye hung around while Mum sorted through his cupboards. He didn't care about clothes that much—on the colony there wasn't much point—but Mum was digging out a whole pile of stuff.

'I quite like that T-shirt,' he said, gruffly.

'This one?'

'Yes.'

Mum put it back without a word. All she said as she went to the door was, 'I hadn't realized how shabby your clothes have been getting, Rye.'

Which wasn't much of a *thank-you*.

* * *

'Rye!'

Mum's voice again. Rye unwillingly opened the door of his room and leant himself against the frame.

'Ah, there you are. This is Stefanie.'

He only threw her the briefest of glances, but it bounced back off her stiff face with almost enough force to hurt.

'We're just walking down to the Hostel. Come and help carry Stefanie's things, will you.'

It was almost the first thing Mum had asked Rye to do since they'd been on the colony: she hardly even said *clean your teeth*. He was so taken aback he couldn't think of a way to get out of it.

There were four carrier bags full of stuff. It seemed to be mostly clothes.

Rye scooped up two bags and led the way grimly down the hill to the Women's Hostel. It wasn't very far, but this was the first time he'd been through the gate.

Mum knocked on the door.

There was a longish pause, and then it opened a little and a woman with a powdery, suspicious face loomed up out of the darkness within. She had coarse tobacco-yellow hair, bandy legs, and her name was painted above the door: *Proprietress Mrs R. Hook*, it said; and the men who drank at the Hostel (which was all of them) joked that her first name was *Right*.

Mum spoke rapidly, so rapidly that she stuttered and fell over her careful Governor's-wife voice. This was Stefanie, who needed somewhere to stay.

Mrs Hook shrugged, and went to close the door; but Mum spoke again. She spoke about gratitude and kindness. Offered money for the girl's keep. Plenty of money.

Mrs Hook ran a black-rimmed and calculating eye over Stefanie and said something about unsuitability and extra work.

Again Rye thought Mum would run away in a hot-faced muddle and a flap; but she seemed to have become very brave, today. She took a huge gulping breath, put a hand protectively on Stefanie's shoulder, and started talking about the granting of licences, and about liquor duty: talked as if she really knew about them, too.

How on earth did Mum know about things like that? Mum didn't know anything.

And then Mrs Hook, the terrifying Mrs Hook, with her face as sour as winceberries, opened the door a little wider. And Mum gave the carrier bags to Stefanie, who stumbled through the door with them and was lost to sight.

Halfway up the hill, Mum suddenly said, 'This is a terrible place.' And although she'd said that a thousand times already, this time it sounded as if she were saying it in a new way.

'I don't think Dad could really help what happened,' said Rye.

Mum looked round and shivered.

'A place needs a god,' she said. 'It's a terrible thing to live in a place without a god.'

They finished their walk in silence. And Rye thought about gods. Ones who dwelt under the deepest caves of the island. And he knew it was time they were worshipped again.

19

B ut Kris didn't want to talk about the offlander gods.

'Look!' he said.

Rye looked.

'It's a seagull,' he said.

'It's an *ice*-gull,' said Kris. 'See the white on the leading edge of the wings?'

'What about it?'

'They're sea-wanderers, ice-gulls. They only come here to breed.'

'Oh. So . . . are they something to do with magic?' Then, when Kris frowned, Rye went on, lightly, 'Are they going to dance an offlander jig with the flat crabs when the moon shines on the third hill to the left of the great Comm Station?'

Kris rolled Rye in the grass and absent-mindedly stuffed scratchy bits of fern down his shirt.

'It means they're laying eggs,' Kris said. '*Eggs!*'

Rye extracted the bits of fern carefully. How long was it since he'd had a fresh egg?

'Where do they nest?' he asked.

'We'll have to watch them, and see.'

The gulls were flying over the brow of the hill, and by the time Rye and Kris reached the blue tape that stretched round it Rye was out of breath.

They paused there. This was prison territory, now, and really seriously out of bounds. But you could see the elegant wings of the gulls tipping upwards as they landed.

The Governor wouldn't find out.

Would he?

Rye shrugged and ducked under the tape.

'What was *that*?' said Kris.

Rye put a foot back to steady himself as the long shuddering passed away. What was it? A tremor of some kind: but not a proper earthquake, because the Governor had always said you didn't get them here.

'One of your earth-shakers,' he said. 'Don't worry. Trust the quench-lizards.'

But Kris's dark head was turning, strangely nervous.

The ground shuddered again, more strongly. It made the ferns rustle around them as if it were full of snakes.

Down in the settlement worried faces would be looking out of their little metal houses.

'We'd better get out of here,' said Rye, reluctantly. If the Governor found out they'd been up beyond the prison boundaries they'd probably end up spending all their free time for a week with a chain gang.

Kris turned back towards the blue tape that marked the perimeter. He went easily over the rough ground, jumping from rock to rock and swerving his hands to avoid the curling, stinging shoots of the new spring ferns. Rye lumbered after him as fast as he could.

When they got near the brow of the hill they threw themselves down and went forward on their stomachs. Below them was the scatter of little houses and service buildings that formed the colony.

'It all looks quiet,' said Rye, cautiously.

He could see Gabriel and Clarissa still clearing the way for the new road, with Hercules driving the dumper; and over by the sea wall a group of intent grey men were working round the warehouse. They couldn't have felt anything.

But there was the Comm Station, bristling with aerials and goodness knows what; it would have picked up the tremor. And it would be reported to the Governor at once.

Now he was still, Rye could feel it again; a long shivering of the earth beneath him, almost as if someone had started a giant motor underground.

Perhaps it was just something to do with the prison. Now that it was occupied, various things had been found wrong with the design, and more excavation was being done. Lisa Shoreman had been coming home every day wheezing with the dust.

'We'll go back down the old river bed,' said Rye.

The river diversion had been a huge job, but the old channel now provided a convenient and almost invisible way down to the settlement.

Rye rolled down into it and pulled his backpack after him carefully. It contained four beautiful large-yolked gull's eggs. You could fry them on a paint tin over a candle, and it worked really well as long as you got the tin properly level first.

He'd have to make sure he remembered to grease the tin, he thought, as he made his way down the pebbly slope. If you didn't the eggs got welded on to the tin and turned to chewy—

And then there was a new vibration that mounted and shivered until his toes were tingling inside his shoes.

'Phew!' he said to Kris. 'That was a big one!' He actually had to stop moving for a minute so he didn't lose his balance. Just for a moment it was like—yes, it was like being on one of those long-ago escalators in a big store on the mainland.

'Rye,' began Kris, suddenly, 'Rye, I think—'

But the vibration was still growing. And it wasn't smooth, now, like an escalator. It became rough, as if it was going over jolting bumps.

Misfiring, thought Rye, which didn't make sense. But then he seemed to have entered a world where things had more or less stopped making sense.

Kris's mouth was moving, but for some reason Rye couldn't make out what he was saying.

It must be a dream, he thought. Except that the air was too fresh for a dream, and the small shocks that came through the soles of his shoes were too sharp and unpredictable. Small fragments of peat began to fall round him from the rim of the channel.

We'd better get out of here, he thought, through the dream-vague unreality of everything. If the channel collapses—

And then there was a sudden shift in the ground under his feet—and he was flying.

20

Rye put out his hands to save himself, but the ground wasn't there any more. There were a dizzy few moments when he didn't know which way up he was, and then he slammed into something that disintegrated as he hit it. The part of his mind that wasn't taken up with complete and utter amazement was slightly aware that he'd been thrown right out of the channel and into a scratch-pea bush.

It really is an earthquake, he thought.

That was the last chance he had to think anything clearly for a long time.

The earth under him was vibrating again. It started so deep, deep down that at first he could only feel it as a quivering in his belly; but then it swelled and came up the scale so that it was like standing by the foghorn on the supply ship. No, it was like two foghorns—like three, like four: and now the noise had picked him up, tossed him aside, shaken the breath out of him, left him curled tight, hands clasped to ears, tiny in the vastness of the hills and fragile, fragile, fragile.

And now there was a rushing of hot air round him, and a metal-smell unlike anything he knew. And when he opened his eyes he found that everything had changed colour.

It was all unreal, a nightmare. The soft browns and greys of the colony had turned to acid crimson; even the air was red, and it was thick, cloying, choking. Rye hauled in a breath, but the air itself was as thick as soup;

he tried to push himself up, but he was too dizzy to know which way up was; he looked around, tried to find a spot of permanence that would stop his head waltzing so crazily.

But even the hillside was dancing.

It was, it really was: the fern and grass was turning and waving and waving.

And waving.

Goodbye, it waved, as it all disappeared so easily. A whole hillside, it was, disappearing so gracefully, so neatly, like a flower folding up at night: it crumpled and caved in slowly, slowly, relentlessly, impossibly. And all Rye could do was watch it, and not believe it, and listen to the long, long rumbling, and the thousand echoes, and the million echoes of echoes.

And then the roaring stopped.

Then there was silence. So much silence. So wide and empty a silence.

And now there was a curtain coming towards Rye. It was a billowing curtain, flounced and blue like the one in the drawing room.

Out of the world, spellbound, Rye watched it come. It came with a multitude of sprouting frills of grey.

It was a little like a forest, Rye sort of thought, groping through the silent ringing of his mind.

It was close, now; and now it was here, with a harsh gash of hot air that brushed him flat. Everything went black, suddenly, except for thousands of brilliant juggling stars that stung like little wasps.

The forest, he thought. *The forest is full of fireflies.*

He found himself quite content, really, except for not being able to breathe properly. Rye wondered vaguely if an owl had wrapped its fuzzy wings around his face. He rolled away from it, fell hard three feet, and found himself back in the channel.

He gasped in three huge mouthfuls of clean air, choked, and coughed and coughed. There was oily grit all over his face and a blinding smart in his eyes.

A little way away, curled into a hollow where the overhang of fern protected the crumbly peat, there was a patch of something furry. But that was impossible. There were no furred animals here. There were pale blotched salamanders that swathed through the fern like bloated hosepipes and raised your skin into blisters if you touched them, but—

Rye hauled in another breath and shook himself into the real world.

'Kris!' he shouted. 'Kris! Are you all right?'

Kris's eyes were amazingly grey. The only grey thing in a world that was red. Everything was red. Their clothes, their skin, the sky, everything.

'What happened?' Kris asked, as if he really thought Rye would know.

Their voices were as tiny and brittle as porcelain crabs.

Rye tried to think. Something had come and changed the whole world: had tossed him about like a leaf and crumbled the hillside into nothingness.

Was there anything left of the world except the two of them?

Rye veered his mind away from that. What had happened?

Rye waited, and his thoughts settled, as slowly and waywardly as the red dust, into some sort of order. Something had caused the hillside over the prison to collapse.

Then the truth hit him, and he gagged on it.

'The prison!' he said. 'Kris, the prison!'

Kris gasped and gaped. Then he scrambled to his feet.

Rye grabbed him.

'Don't,' he said. 'Stay here. It may not have finished.'

But Kris had shaken himself free and was already clambering out over the ferny overhang. Rye cursed and hauled himself out after him. All he could see was confusing swirling drifts of red fog. But Rye could hear, through his still ringing ears, Kris's tiny, tinny voice.

'Mum!' it was shouting. *'Mum!'*

21

The blue tape that had marked the perimeter of the prison had disappeared from the face of the earth. Rye looked around, hesitated, and then forced his legs uphill.

There wasn't an uphill for long. The fern at his feet quickly turned black, and then two steps later there were only scanty twists of charcoal that cracked into dust under his feet.

And then there was nothing.

Really nothing.

No fern, no earth, just swirling red and billowing grey going down for ever.

Like a huge cauldron, thought Rye, in the far down part of his brain that was still sort of working. Half an hour ago it had been a hill that had been there for ever: and now it was nothing.

Rye turned aside and stumbled on as fast as he could. It wasn't easy: he couldn't see far, and there were big pieces of earth and rock that had cracked away from the rest and were hanging onto the edge of the crater by just a few roots.

It was hard to get his bearings. Half the things were so covered in red dust that he couldn't recognize them, and the other half had been blown away, or buried under tons and tons of rubble.

Am I the only one left? Rye thought, and faltered. Perhaps he'd somehow got turned round and was running away from the colony up into the hills.

And then in front of him something moved. It was huge and broad and dark, and it was only at that moment that Rye realized how frightened he was.

Rye was about to turn and run when the thing emerged from a cloud of smoke and turned from a wraith into a giant with shining eyes.

Rye threw himself forward.

'Gabriel!'

The man steadied himself, and then steadied Rye.

'Rye? That you, under all that dust?'

Rye clutched at Gabriel's arm.

'It blew up,' he said. 'The prison. And the hill's gone. The top's blown off.'

'I know. I know, Rye. Come on down this way, now.'

It was only a little way down to the stone-packed mud of a track. But which track was it? Everything seemed to have been thrown in the air and scrunched, and Rye had almost given up expecting things to join up as they used to. But this must be—yes, this was the track up to the prison entrance. Only now it was a track leading up to a mountain of earth and rubble.

Clarissa was there, ticking and purring.

'I'm going to work fast, now, Rye, so you keep clear, OK? I don't want to have to worry about you getting under our tracks.'

The smoke was curdling, now, allowing Rye sudden unexpected views along sweeping corridors of red dusty air. Gabriel pulled a curiously bright handkerchief out of his pocket and wrapped it round his face.

Everything had been turned upside down, inside out, back to front: all the world was filthy and red, and the only clean thing anywhere was a road-maker's handkerchief.

Clarissa coughed and choked into motion and began to bump her way across the rock-strewn road towards the mountain of rubble that had once been the prison.

The prison.

'Blooming pirates,' Murray had complained only yesterday. 'Now this new bloke's turned up he's unsettled the lot of them.'

'Thinks he's god,' said Lotty, lugubriously. 'Got 'em all marching backwards and forwards from dawn till dusk, poor blighters.'

'And we were getting quite friendly,' said Murray, offended. 'But now—they *won't* talk, they *don't* gamble, they flipping *sleep* at attention . . . too good for us, now, they are. And it's not as if they were the only ones in for serious crimes, not by a long chalk.'

Where was Murray?

Please, thought Rye, *please*—but he wasn't sure if the gods would listen to him.

Now the smoke was drifting into another clear view. And there—thank all the gods.

'Kris!'

Kris's hair was completely red, and there were crusts round his mouth. He was a little way up the rubble mountain and he was grubbing up handfuls of debris and throwing them out of the way.

Rye ran across and clambered and flailed up to him.

'Gabriel's brought Clarissa up,' he said. 'He'll shift the stuff a million times faster than you. Come down out of the way.'

But Kris only scooped up another handful of rock. His thumb was bleeding already.

'My mum's in there,' he said.

Lisa Shoreman, and Lotty with his rheumatism, and Murray with his embroidery, and more than a hundred others.

Rye looked round helplessly and saw something poking up through the jumble of rubble. He slithered over to it and pulled.

It was a piece of plasterboard, the stuff that was used for the inside walls of buildings. Rye tried not to imagine what it was doing there. Buildings were supposed to be for ever. That was one of the things about living on a new colony: you built things. It wasn't all supposed to disintegrate into nothing again.

And here was another piece of board. Rye tugged it and hauled on it and got it free at last. It would have been easier to dig it out, but Rye didn't want to find out what was underneath it.

What was that? someone had thought.

And then the sky had fallen on them.

'Here,' said Rye. 'Load the stuff on to boards and drag it away. It'll be faster.'

Working stopped you having time to think. Loading the spoil, dragging it out of the way, going back for more, with all the time the red dust getting up your nose and in your mouth until the whole world tasted bitter.

Other people were arriving with spades and trucks, now. Even the gaudy women came, and set to work in strange grim silence. Rye and Kris loaded their boards, dragged them down to the road, and the men shovelled the earth up on to the trucks. Harry Shoreman came with the spade he used for his vegetable plot. Everything was confused and haphazard to start with, but after a while the trucks were organized so that each could do its job without hampering the others. The rubble mountain, that had been nibbled at inefficiently from all directions, causing minor rock-falls and delay, began to retreat. The mood of the workers lifted from dull confusion into something exceedingly purposeful.

'Rye!'

Rye had been waiting for that voice. He tried pretending not to hear, but one of the men—which one, the gods only knew, for he was red and black like all the rest—touched his shoulder.

'Governor wants you, Rye.'

And Rye sighed, surrendered his board to whoever-it-was, and tiptoed and slid his way off the rubble and down to the road.

The Governor was standing, hands on his hips, directing operations. He was covered in red dust just like everything else, but somehow in his case it added to his dignity, almost turned him into a statue of himself: *The First Governor*.

'I need a messenger,' said the Governor. 'Here's a note for the Comm Station. Now go.'

Rye went.

22

Jogging down the track jarred Rye's overworked joints. The dust had smeared itself into a smog that hung sullenly, now, making everything seem sinister and unfamiliar.

And then the washing-line posts outside the Women's Hostel loomed into view; and that made his heart sink even further because it meant he'd come too far. How on earth, even allowing for all the smoke and smog, had he managed to miss the Comm Station?

The journey back up the hill was really hard work: he was dead tired, and the rescue effort up at the prison was constantly stirring up more dust that twirled elegantly down the hill to get in his mouth and prickle his skin. Then something dark appeared to his left, and Rye stopped. It looked like the electricity plant; but, of course, it couldn't be, because that meant he'd have missed the Comm Station again.

He turned off the track anyway and ploughed through the long wet grass towards the fuzzy block of darker smog.

He didn't believe it until he had to: it was only a trick of the smoke, or of the lowering dusk. Or it was something magnified by the smog: a wheelbarrow; or a hut that had been shaken from its place and juddered down the hill; or a new building only erected that afternoon.

Then he saw the chain-link fence and his heart bumped. Every line and knot of wire was softened with red dust. But he still didn't believe it until he'd taken three more steps, and he was sure.

There was a sign a couple of yards downhill. It said:

DANGER: HIGH VOLTAGE ELECTRICITY.
STRICTLY NO ADMITTANCE
BY ORDER OF THE GOVERNOR.

Rye hooked his fingers through the wire and gazed at the cube of tubes and metal. As long as he was thinking about that, he wasn't thinking about anything else. So he thought hard about the electricity plant. How it worked. How Gabriel had let Rye take control of Clarissa when he was clearing the site. How smoothly and easily the joysticks moved the bucket. The complete joy of being part of Clarissa, of seeing her respond to his touch. Of building things.

But Clarissa had cleared another site near here.

Rye turned left along the fence. He didn't want to go because he knew what he was going to find.

Or not going to find.

He came across the main mast first. The huge cables that had held it up had splayed and bunched beneath it, so it jutted out a few feet off the ground.

The way's blocked, thought Rye: but that was only an excuse. He put a heavy knee up on the mast and heaved himself clumsily across.

The Comm Station was the only tall structure on the colony. It had been made of wooden panels and girders, and it had collapsed like a card house. The wreckage of masts and cables spread across the ground at ugly, unbalanced angles. There was an electric hum from somewhere close: it spluttered occasionally, as if it were choking.

Rye stood and was afraid. He listened. There were gulls mewing, and the electric hum, and Clarissa, and the shovelling of tons of earth. But all those sounds seemed suddenly far away, and there was only himself, breathing, and the silence from the Comm Station.

The man in charge of the Comm Station, Mr Peabody, had a beard, and very white teeth, and an anchor tattooed on his arm.

Rye gathered all his courage.

'Hello!' he called. But his voice was knocked down flat by the smog. That made him angry, so he said it louder.

'Hello! Hello!'

What if there was an answer? Someone might shout they were trapped. They might be in pain, disfigured, dying. They might be dying.

But there was no answer, and Rye felt something rise inside him that was horribly like relief.

But no, no, he didn't want everybody to be dead. He didn't, he didn't. Not Mr Peabody, or Stanley, or Ned.

Definitely not Ned, who could make stones turn into shells and then turn them back again with a flick of his handkerchief right in front of your eyes.

Rye suddenly couldn't stand it.

'Where are you?' he shouted, angrily.

No one answered.

23

People were still labouring as Rye stumbled across the trampled grass. Kris was tugging his loaded board down the rubble mountain yet again, even though he was so tired that his legs would no longer carry him reliably in a straight line.

What if it was my mother in there? thought Rye. But he couldn't imagine it.

Everyone was here, even the girl from the Women's Hostel. She was carrying water to the rescuers.

Rye turned wearily towards the only figure that was still strong, was still upright, was still in control.

And then there was a flat explosion and almost instantly its echo: bank-*bank*.

Rye stopped.

People were running towards him, stumbling outwards from the rubble mountain like tumbled dice.

And now a pillow of smoke was bursting its way outwards behind them. Gabriel was scrambling out of Clarissa's cabin and vaulting down and away. The smoke was exploding outwards in a bulging cauliflower-barrier, snatching the little figures, blotting them out. It made its way on tiny delicate fingers, but fast, fast; and while Rye wavered, it was on him.

Everything vanished. Instantly. Rye stumbled forward on invisible feet, tripped over something, and fell.

The smoke was choke-thick, but it was moving, rolling up and away and letting the sweet air in underneath it.

And then it had gone.

All over the hillside people were pushing themselves ever-so-wearily to their feet. But now they were smiling, and cheering, and waving tired arms in the air. Because there was a whole crowd of bright people at the foot of the rubble mountain. Everyone and everything else on the hillside was covered in layer after layer of clinging red dust, but these people were clean and bright, and there was a dark hole in the rubble behind them.

They had blown their way through the rubble. From *inside* the prison.

Perhaps they're alive, thought Rye, his heart somersaulting painfully. And he began to run. Kris was stumbling down the rubble from the other side of the rescue site.

Now someone else was appearing in the opening that had appeared in the rubble. He was stepping carefully, heavily, holding the wooden handles of a stretcher.

Rye's heart went over another bump.

Someone hurt.

Hurt, like at the Comm Station.

'Rye!'

The Governor wasn't filthy like everyone else: he'd been standing so grandly, directing operations, that the dust had fallen over him evenly and gently and turned him into something like an over-stuffed velvet sofa. Only his bright eyes moved. They darted everywhere and missed nothing.

He took in a deep breath at Rye's news.

'That's most unfortunate,' he said. 'Extremely unfortunate. A great loss.'

Another stretcher was just beginning to be visible in the darkness of the tunnel. There was a woman on this one. She wore the dark uniform of a prison warder. Her white-blonde hair had twisted itself loose.

Rye felt as if someone had punched him hard in the stomach. He couldn't breathe at all for a long time, but then he took in a long difficult breath and managed to find a bit of his voice.

'That's Kris's mum,' he said.

Kris was walking alongside the stretcher, and Harry Shoreman was taking the handles at the back anxiously, gently, urgently.

When the stretcher came near, Rye made himself speak.

'Kris, is she—how is she?'

But Kris wouldn't look at Rye. He plunged past, one hand protectively on the rail of the stretcher. The men turned to carry it down the track, and Kris went with it.

Rye ran errands until the dusk thickened the air impossibly and the worst news had come up from the rescue team down at the Comm Station. By then all but a handful of the prisoners had been brought out and chained together and taken to a hastily-fenced holding area. Neither Kris nor his father returned, but the girl from the Hostel carried on silently right to the end.

Rye went down to the shore, to a place where the river had swirled a deep hole in the purple mudflats, and swam until he'd washed all the red dust away.

He got home before the Governor.

24

There were no more tremors in the night. The moon rose hugely, palely, above the mudflats, and brought with it a torrent of water, twisting and chuckling over the mud, bathing millions upon millions of tiny creatures. Worms blossomed delicate gills and anemones oozed hungry tentacles. A million million crabs danced, tipped backwards to balance the weight of their ridiculous claws. The red dust that still fell, piling in drifts round the corners of buildings, was on the sea whirled into swirls of scum, waterlogged, and sunk into oblivion.

Rye lay and prayed for nearly a minute before he fell asleep.

There was never really a dawn on the colony, even when the air was not thick with falling dust. It got lighter, but slowly and grudgingly. Every so often, if you were lucky, the cloud might thin enough for the shrouded sun to cast faint shadows. But that was only if you were lucky.

Rye dressed to the clank of machinery and the windy *hwoof-hwoofing* that filled every early morning. Nothing was going to stop the Governor keeping fit. Nothing: not ten people dead and still some missing; not Lisa Shoreman borne away on a stretcher; not the colony cut off from help, and all the island trembling on the edge of ruin. Nothing short of the end of the world: if this were not the end of the world already.

Mum looked like death.

'I suppose Rye can't do lessons today,' she said, sitting, rigid, but somehow collapsed, in front of her unused plate. 'Not if we can't get through to the mainland.'

The Governor's head shook above its cushions of chins.

'Indeed not. I'll be needing Willis, in any case. We'll be starting the salvage operation, getting things tidied up. Back to normal.'

Rye blinked away the thought of what they might be tidying up.

The Governor was bathed and shaved and bandbox neat; but perhaps the lines about his mouth were even more determined.

He shoved rather a lot of marmalade-glistening toast into his mouth.

'But you can help your mother, Rye,' he said, once he'd cement-mixered it all down. 'Take some sheets and blankets to the medicentre.'

Mum raised a wan face.

'But should Rye go out, Ryland? If there's another tremor—'

'Then he's better off outside,' said the Governor, brusquely.

So Rye hung around until Mum had loaded him up with a heap of worn and mildewy sheets and several eccentrically hand-knitted blankets, and went out at last with Mum's cautions about after-shocks clinging to him.

The medicentre had only come into being yesterday. It had been the administration building of the old prison before that, and it still lurked greyly behind barbed wire.

There were prison warders on the gate. They weren't letting anyone in, or releasing details about the injured, but Joe Bruce agreed to enquire about Lisa. She was suffering from dust-inhalation, but was as well as could be expected. That was as much as he could say.

Rye took the news up to the food stall, but it was shut

up. The Shoremans' house was deserted, too, and the prisoners were all fenced off and out of reach.

He made his way back down to the settlement the long way, the way that didn't take him past the Comm Station. There was a figure standing by the gate to the Women's Hostel. He was going to walk past, but it called him.

'Excuse me,' it said. Which wasn't the sort of thing people on the colony usually said.

Rye stopped at a safe distance. The girl's hair was scraped into two short plaits that stuck out behind her like a frigate-bird's tail, and her face was dead, dead white: as white as Mum's had been this morning.

He wanted to say, *What do you want?*

The words came out of her as if they were being forced out under pressure.

'I was wondering . . . do you know how to . . . how to find out about . . . about who was hurt, yesterday?'

She stammered as if she were nervous, but it wasn't nerves at all: she was in some other state that involved desperate fear and huge amounts of bottled-up resentment.

Rye considered. Those who were hurt were at the medicentre. He didn't know what had happened to those who had died, because it was one of the things he had been careful not to find out.

He could ask the Governor; but the Governor was hugely busy already, and would be bound to publish a list as soon as it could be completed.

The girl was standing stiffly, and her brown eyes were burning in her cold face. She really hated him, Rye realized, suddenly.

That was interesting. Why?

Robin Willis had access to all the files. He would know if anyone did.

'I might be able to find out for you,' Rye offered, quite

99

generously, he thought. 'Was there anyone in particular you wanted to know about?'

She clenched her hands.

'John Arne.'

No one he knew. And that was quite strange, because there were very few people on the colony he didn't know. Must be one of the new intake.

Then Rye had a terrible thought.

'He wasn't the new man at the Comm Station, was he?'

'No,' said the girl. 'No. He was in the caves.'

Rye breathed more freely.

'There weren't that many staff hurt in the caves,' he said. 'There was a group of engineers, and three warders; but none of them was called John. I'm sure none of them was.'

She stood even straighter, and glared at him, her eyes dark with the deepest contempt.

'But my father is a prisoner,' she said.

25

Robin Willis didn't get home until it was nearly dark. He was paler than ever, and blinking, and Rye had to ask him his question three times before he took it in.

'I don't know,' he said. 'I've been over at the Comm Station all day. I don't think the lists are complete. I think they're still digging in the caves.'

The centre of the tremor had been to the south of the occupied parts—it looked as though diverting the river through that soft stratum of rock had set the whole thing off—but there had been major rock falls throughout the system.

'I wanted to find out about a man called John Arne,' persisted Rye.

Robin Willis frowned.

'Arne? Where have I—? Oh. There's a man called Arne in the medicentre.'

Rye gasped. 'Badly hurt?'

'What? Oh, no, no. He's working there. I don't think he's a doctor, but he must have some medical experience. He's one of the prisoners, of course, but we need all the help we can get just at the moment.'

Mum hurried anxiously along the corridor from the kitchen.

'Has something else happened?' she asked. 'Robin, what is it?'

'Nothing, Mrs Makepeace. Everything's . . . the same. It's just been a long day, that's all.'

'You'll need your tea, then. I got them to leave some things out for you.'

The table was covered with the ice-patterned cloth and the little fancy pots.

Robin Willis sat down and stared at it as if he didn't know what it was for.

Rye walked down into the centre of the settlement.

Rye knew all the women who lived at the Hostel. They were all very pretty—except Mrs Hook—and very friendly—also except Mrs Hook—but the place made him uncomfortable.

So he was glad to see Annie sitting on the doorstep, reading. Annie was easily his best friend among the Hostel women: she was always properly interested in what he had to say, and she enjoyed watching Clarissa almost as much as Rye did. And though, of course, everyone loved Gabriel, it was Annie who always made sure he had something sustaining to eat for his lunch.

'I've come out here for some peace and quiet,' Annie said, when she'd called back into the house for the girl. 'None of us can settle to anything. We're all still quivering: and we ripped our hands to shreds shifting rubble yesterday. We all look like old washer-women.'

'Your hands'll soon heal up,' said Rye.

She looked up at him, and then she suddenly smiled.

'Of course they will. I'm sorry, Rye, of course it doesn't matter, really. I'm just truly grateful to be still breathing. Better people than me aren't.'

The girl loomed palely into sight against the darkness of the doorway and Rye saw the wave of fear that washed across her when she saw him; but then she stiffened her face into neutral again.

'Here's Rye for you, Steff.'

The girl came out and down the path, but she stopped a little way from him. She was clutching a dishmop, and Rye suddenly felt sorry for her.

'I've found out about your father,' he said. 'He's all right. He's fine, not hurt at all. He's helping at the medicentre.'

She went pink, then, absolutely suddenly.

'Thank you,' she said; but the words clattered meaninglessly on the ground between them.

Rye shrugged, and walked away.

26

The Governor reached his garden gate as dusk was settling. He was walking briskly, and flourishing behind him a glorious train of sunset-coloured dust.

Havers the butler saw him coming, put down the sugar-bowl he was polishing, and made dignified haste to hold open the front door.

But the Governor didn't get there. Halfway down the path he staggered, and after two more steps he went down onto his hands and knees. By the time Havers and Charlie Box had got to him, he was as limp on the ground as a beached whale.

The commotion brought Rye out of his room. He was in time to see them, half-distracted with fright and incredulity, dragging the Governor into the house. Everyone was panicking: Robin Willis was rushing backwards and forwards, Teresa the cook was flapping a tea towel about, and Miss Last was sitting down in a corner, elegant, but not conscious.

'A doctor,' cried Mum. 'For pity's sake, someone, get a doctor!'

And Robin Willis rushed out and was halfway down the path before anybody would listen to Rye telling them that there wasn't a doctor any more.

'He's still breathing,' said Charlie Box. 'He's still breathing!'

Rye blundered away from the lot of them so he could think. There was no doctor, so who could help? But that was easy: the man who helped everyone when they were ill.

So where would Harry Shoreman be? His house had been shut up. Would he be at the caves? Or off doing magic in the dark hills?

Well, Rye would just have to look, that was all. And keep looking, until he found him.

Rye opened the door—and then he saw something: something was lying on the path.

His stomach did a clumsy somersault. He stepped out and went over to look.

It was only a frond of fern, but it was twisted together in a surprising way.

Rye picked it up and opened it out.

There was a piece of root inside. It smelt familiar. What was that smell? What *was* it?

Yes. It was the scent of the winter hills: of scratch-pea bloom.

You can make a curse with the root, Kris had said.

An offlander curse.

Harry?

Kris?

Rye stood with the thing in his hands and felt very cold, and very sad. Then he put the root carefully back inside the fern frond and put the whole thing into his pocket. He hesitated, listening to the wailing in the house behind him; but then he began to jog after Robin Willis down towards the settlement.

The news about the Governor was there before him. Men were spilling out of the Hostel with glasses in their hands to stare up at the lights of the Governor's house. *Heart attack*, some people were saying; *a stroke*, said others. Rye went through them until he found the biggest, broadest figure of them all.

'Gabriel!'

Gabriel jumped at the sound of Rye's voice.

'Rye! What are you doing down here so late?' he asked;

but his eyes were full of worry and pity, and he put a huge arm round Rye's shoulders.

'Look,' said Rye, and showed Gabriel the curse. 'I think this is what's wrong with Dad. I think he collapsed when he stepped over it.'

Gabriel caught his breath at the sight of it.

'May the great gods protect us,' he said, softly. 'All right. It's all right, now, Rye. Wait here, I won't be long. We need an expert in this sort of thing.'

Mrs Hook glared at Rye as if he were responsible for the curse himself. Then she poked her large powdery nose over the root and sniffed at it violently.

'Scratch-pea,' she announced, with certainty and scorn. 'Amateur stuff, that is. That'll fade as the root rots, in any case.'

'But it's the Governor, ma'am,' said Gabriel, steadily. 'We can't manage without him.' And Mrs Hook sniffed again.

'I suppose in that case we'd better get it sorted out straight away,' she conceded. 'Where is he, now? And his lady, is she with him? We'll need her, too.'

And she strode powerfully back up the hill to the Governor's house.

Dad was still unconscious, and his eyes showed ghostly crescents of white. Mum was cradling his head and stroking his hair and murmuring words Dad couldn't hear.

'You've got to come,' Rye told her. 'It's important. You've got to come.'

Mum hardly seemed to know where she was, but she gave a little gasping scream when she saw the curse.

'Oh, thank all the gods,' she said, going white, then red, then white again. 'Oh, bless us all.'

'Do you know what to do, ma'am?' asked Mrs Hook, cocking a bright eye at her. 'Have you seen something like it before?' And Mum gaped, and hesitated. But then she snatched up the twisted root and began rubbing it fiercely between her hands, faster and faster, until the warm scent gushed out and filled the room, like flowers, but also like the acid smell of salamanders.

'*Now*,' snapped Mrs Hook: and Mum threw down the root and stamped on it hard.

It split with a small popping sound, and the scent blossomed, turned rotten, and vanished.

And from the room across the corridor, where Miss Last was tiptoeing around dabbing a lavender-scented handkerchief on the Governor's brow, an irritable and perfectly awake voice said: '*Whatever do you think you're doing, Miss Last?*'

No one could ever explain to Rye just how the fight outside the Hostel started that night—it was quite probable that no one really knew—but the noise of it reached the Governor's house before Miss Last had twittered her way to the end of an explanation.

'Nonsense!' snapped the Governor, heaving himself up. 'What's that commotion?' And he sailed, magnificent and lavender-scented, and with Mrs Hook at his right hand, down the hill.

The people on the outskirts of the fight saw them coming and ran for it; but Mrs Hook's white stiletto shoe caught young Kevin Frost and sent him right across the road; and Dicky Paton found himself somehow in the ditch with a ringing head and a thick ear. The Governor stood, arms akimbo, in the light from the windows, and glared until everyone who was left had shrunk to the size of earwigs and crawled humbly away. Then the Governor nodded, shook hands with Mrs Hook, and went home to supper.

'How did you know what to do?' Rye asked Mum, much later.

'Oh, it was only a simple curse, Rye,' she said. 'It was silly of me to get into a tizz. I should have thought of it at once when I saw Dad's eyes.'

'So . . . it was magic,' said Rye, to get things straight.

'Yes, of course it was, my love.'

'Do you know any more?' Rye asked, wistfully.

'Magic? Lord love you, no. That's not for the likes of me.'

'But you could break the curse,' persisted Rye.

Mum looked at him, puzzled.

'Well, yes,' she said. 'But I can squish a wasp, can't I, but it doesn't mean I can make one from scratch. Doesn't mean I understand it. That's what magic is, Rye. Things people don't understand.'

If it hadn't been Mum who had said it, Rye might have thought that was wise.

'I suppose that's why it's not in the Prescribed Schedules,' he said.

'That's why most things aren't in the Prescribed Schedules,' said Mum.

27

Despite no one's being allowed into the medicentre, everyone knew that people weren't getting better as fast as they should have been. Lisa Shoreman had been taken home, but Harry's food stall was still shut up. It was said that he had been digging in a tiger-ant nest for ingredients for a spell, and that it was taking all his magic to keep her going.

People were beginning to talk about poisonous fumes.

Rye went and knocked at the Shoremans' house; but no one answered, even though someone was coughing inside. On the doorstep were a bunch of pale orchids and a dried-up thing that looked uncomfortably as if it might once have been a frog.

Magic.

Rye went away feeling smaller than ever.

On the second day after the quake Rye was chased away from his CAD system by a whirlwind of Teresa-wielded duster. So he walked down to the settlement until he came across Gabriel and Clarissa digging a trench. By some freak of the weather it actually hadn't rained for several days, and the red dust rose round them and clung smotheringly to everything, so that even Clarissa's gleaming paintwork was dimmed. Rye sat on the slope a little way above them to watch. Gabriel was working with great care and unusual sobriety, digging and spinning and letting fall the soil, and not singing at all.

'Hey!' came a shrill voice. 'Hey-hey-hey!'

Clarissa stopped in mid-swing, and her engine lowered to an easy chuntering.

'Hercules? You all right?'

Hercules's head appeared. It jerked in the direction of the trench. Gabriel pulled aside his armrest and jumped down.

They all peered into the hole together.

'Gods above,' breathed Gabriel, after a long time. 'Gods above, there's people here already.'

Then he remembered Rye and turned on him.

'Rye! What are you doing here? You shouldn't be hanging around, it's not respectful. Go and find the Governor, and tell him . . . tell him—'

'That the grave you are digging is already filled with bodies,' said Rye, hardly able to believe it.

It was only the skulls, he could see, really. Clarissa had turned up perhaps half a dozen of them, arranged in a deep layer of black charcoal ash. The nearest one had been crushed by Clarissa's bucket; and so had that one over there; and even that one, which was too deep in the earth for Clarissa to have damaged, was dinted.

They'd all been crushed. That one looked as if it had been hit with an axe.

'Rye!' said Gabriel, scandalized.

And Rye took one last look, and went.

It turned out it was only the skulls that were buried.

'Some primitive ritual,' said the Governor, acidly, during a brief visit home. 'I imagine they crushed the craniums in order to release the souls of the dead; or to exterminate vengeful spirits; or to appease their gods. Some nonsense.'

Aranui, Aranui,
Netter of souls . . .

110

'What are you going to do with them?' asked Rye.

'I was *going* to have them reburied; but someone's come in the night and taken the lot of them.'

Rye almost wished he'd thought of doing that himself.

'I wonder what they wanted them for?' asked Mum, soberly.

'Who can say? Well, probably Harry Shoreman could: no doubt they're his relatives, and I expect it's he who's got them. Some of his magical mumbo-jumbo.'

The Governor had been forced to accept that he had collapsed the night before, but he was putting it down to lack of nourishment. No one had dared mention the curse.

'Well, I expect Harry knows where they'll be happiest,' said Mum.

'Nonsense! Superstitious nonsense. It's a criminal offence, and I shall certainly pursue the matter. I'll be sorting out Harry Shoreman and his son in my own good time.'

The Governor wore a black shiny tie for the funerals, and Rye shuddered at his forethought. Rye stood with Mum. She cried quite a lot, but it seemed only right.

Seven prisoners and seven colonists, put in bags and into the ground.

The Governor addressed everyone at the endless end of the ceremony.

'My dear friends,' he said. 'These are testing times for us. Hard times. Sad times. But we will support each other to better ones.'

And, incredibly, people went their separate ways more hopeful, as if the Governor could stop any more earthquakes; as if it wasn't he who was responsible for all the deaths in the first place.

Robin Willis staggered back to the Comm Station. He knew more about communications systems than anyone else left in the colony and the Governor had made it clear it was his responsibility to get it all working again. The supply ship wasn't due for three months.

Mum went home to finish her weeping, and Gabriel began the melancholy job of filling in the graves. Rye, very lonely, trudged up to the Shoremans' house; but no one answered when he knocked, even though there was a bowl of escaping copper-worms abandoned on the doorstep.

So he walked across towards the prison to see how the work was going on. It was still a shock to find that the short cut over the hill led you to the vast cauldron of the crater. Rye went to the edge and peered down over the jumble of rubble.

There was something down there: a big bundle of red cloth that hung on a bit of rope from a spur of rock. It was hardly dusty at all, so it could only have been put there very recently.

It was probably just reachable.

Rye lay down on his stomach, but he could only just touch the rope with his fingertips. So he perched on the very edge of the crater and tried to hook his foot underneath it.

It almost worked. He got a loop round the toe of his shoe; but the bundle was heavier than he'd thought, and he'd only lifted it a few inches nearer his hand when the thing bent down the soft leather and slipped away.

The instinct to grab was so strong that Rye nearly went after it. He threw himself backwards, his heart thumping high inside his ribs as the cloth bundle bounced down and down.

It split open on the third bounce. Some things must have fallen out of sight between the rocks, but Rye could see a piece of glinting black obsidian; and a razor shell;

and one of those mould-balls that turned the ferns brown and brittle; and what was probably the long ribcage tunnel of a snake; and something withered that must once have been a rare moon-flower.

Rye looked back down towards the Shoremans' house: no sign of anyone, thank all the gods.

He made himself scarce.

'Mum,' said Rye, very casually, after lunch. 'If you found a spell, and broke it all to pieces, would that stop the magic?'

Mum finished counting her stitches.

'I don't know, Rye, love,' she said. 'That would probably depend on who did the spell. A properly laid spell wouldn't be so easy to spoil, I wouldn't think.'

'Oh,' said Rye. 'Er . . . do you know much about ingredients for spells?'

Mum looked at him.

'What have you been meddling with?'

'Nothing,' said Rye. 'It was an accident. It had things like dead snakes in.'

'Well, I just hope you washed your hands, Rye, love.'

'I didn't touch it. And there was a bit of obsidian in it, as well. And a moon-flower.'

'Oh,' said Mum, a little startled. 'A moon-flower. Was there?'

'They're really rare, aren't they? Does that mean something?'

'Well, they say a moon-flower's a sort of timer: it stops the spell going off straight away—it sort of waits until the best time to go off. That'd be a special sort of spell, that would. Something powerful.'

'Oh,' said Rye.

28

E ven now, with half the hillside crumbled into ruin, you could still just about clamber your way to the hill above the prison. Rye ploughed up the hill, hoping for a sight of Gabriel and Clarissa. He wanted to talk to Gabriel, and he had a perfect excuse because he'd had an idea about Clarissa's dust-filtration system. And even if Gabriel was unreachable, then perhaps Rye could get to the prisoners' holding-area and have a chat with Murray or someone: find out how everybody was.

But he found they were already moving the prisoners back into the caves. A green-armbanded contingent was marching in briskly, proudly, like soldiers, and the rest were ambling and shuffling and kicking up the dust while the warders prowled along watchfully beside them.

But then one of the last prisoners, a short man, stopped in front of the entrance, and this brought the ragged procession behind him to a halt. Rye was too far away to see what was happening properly, but he was sure that was Murray. What did Murray think he was doing? His principle had always been to keep his head down and do his time quietly.

One of the warders—Mr Bruce, it was—was shouting orders, now, and the other prisoners were moving on; but Murray's bowed figure didn't move.

The warders looked round, as if for instructions, and it was only then that Rye realized the Governor was there. But where was Lotty? Those two were such a couple: Murray was always getting into a state about something, but Lotty would always manage to calm him—

And then Rye suddenly remembered the long bags that Gabriel had buried, obliterated, with tons of soil.

Joe Bruce walked up to Murray and gave him a push. It sent Murray forward a step.

The next push was harder, and Murray went down onto his hands and knees.

Then Joe got out his baton.

The Governor stood and watched until the last prisoner was in the cave and the gates had been shut. Then he went away.

Rye hid, shivering, behind a boulder until he'd passed.

Rye got back to the settlement feeling so alone that when he saw the girl poking about on the shoreline he even went over to warn her about the mud.

'It's just this bit round here,' he explained. 'The current sets round it and you can gain a foot of depth in just a few seconds.'

She didn't smile, or say thank you; but then he wasn't really expecting her to. Rye sighed, and was about to go off to leave her to drown, when he noticed the great dark stain down the front of her T-shirt.

His T-shirt, actually.

Then he realized that it was blood.

'What have you done to yourself?' he asked; but she only glared at him.

'It's nothing.'

Nothing? He could see the stain spreading as he looked.

'Nonsense,' he said, exactly as the Governor would have done. 'You've cut yourself really badly. Let me see.'

But she stepped back away from him. She practically bared her teeth.

'Leave me alone, Ryland Makepeace!'

Rye wavered. She was bleeding really quite badly. He ought to take her back to the Hostel, except that might involve having to touch her.

'I can't leave you here to bleed to death,' he said, at last, exasperated.

'Much as you'd like to.'

'Much as I'd— Look, just go back home, all right?'

He watched her until she was back on the main track, and he worried about her just slightly for the next couple of days until he saw her on one of the hilltops above the settlement. She was building a cairn from bits of rock.

She jumped when she saw him.

'Is your arm all right now?' he asked, gruffly.

'Yes. Thank you. I must have caught it on a shell or something.'

A bit of bandage showed at her wrist. It criss-crossed itself neatly, like a fancy loaf.

'It looks as if they made a good job of it,' said Rye, politely.

'Yes.'

She had fitted the irregular stones of the cairn together with great care. Whatever it was for.

'What are you making?' he asked, very curious, even though he knew quite well he was asking for trouble.

She turned to face him full on, and for the first time he saw her smile. It made her look quite, quite mad.

'A love-spell house,' she said.

He fled.

Rye, unnerved, went back down to the settlement, but he wandered round the whole place twice before he found

116

Annie sitting reading on the sea wall. Gabriel was still working out of bounds on the prison site, and so she was as glad of someone to talk to as Rye was.

'Thanks for taking care of Steff the other day,' she said, making room for him. 'Six stitches, she had to have, but she was ever so brave. The orderly gave her a little wooden box as a reward, but of course the first thing she did was go and lose it. Poor little thing. She's so surly and rude, but it's only because she's so unhappy.'

There was a storm brewing, everyone kept saying, even though the clouds were white and high and hardly moving. But still everyone shook their heads and chewed ease-root for their headaches, and waited for the storm. Everyone was short-tempered except for Gabriel, who was almost always at the prison, and Kris, who wasn't answering his door. Teresa and Mum were in a frenzy of constant dusting, and the Governor was out supervising the investigation into the new underground course of the river. In the end Rye got so lonely he was reduced to going fishing.

'Bacon?' said Mum, taken aback. 'What are you up to?'

'Just a little bit. It's the best bait you can have. Honestly.'

'I wish we had eggs,' mused Mum, wistfully, ringing the bell.

But the ice-gulls were gone—roasted in the explosion or flown away.

'We'll have crab tonight,' Rye promised.

He went down to the place where the main drain discharged into the sea. All you had to do was tie the bacon on a bit of line and chuck it into one of the channels that meandered through the mounds of purple mud.

117

Within a few minutes the line was unwieldy with saucer-sized flat crabs clinging greedily to the bits of bacon.

Rye stacked the crabs on their backs in a bucket. Then he heaved the whole dour-mouthed, claw-waving heap back home.

It was Havers's afternoon off; Charlie Box was concocting a new sort of slug bait that included porridge and chokewort; and Teresa had charged off in search of scale-parsley to make dinner slightly less dull. Miss Last was tapping away busily in her cubicle at volume seven of her romantic novel and wasn't to be disturbed.

'Just you and me,' said Mum, very pleased. 'We'll have a proper feast with this lot. Oh lord, look, Rye, their feelers are green as grass. They're not supposed to be like that, are they?'

'Lots of them are at the moment,' said Rye. 'But it's all right, I've cooked crabs with green antennae loads of times.'

Mum gave him a sideways look.

'Have you?' she said. 'Where was that, then? On the beach, in a paint tin, over an open fire?'

'We could have a picnic,' said Rye, suddenly missing Kris very much.

Mum pushed back one of the honey-coloured tendrils of hair that was clinging to her red face.

'Dad wouldn't want me sitting about eating crabs with my fingers, Rye. And anyway, it wouldn't be right, when things are so sad.'

'An indoor picnic, then,' Rye said. 'We could sit on a blanket by the window. No one would see you there.'

And no one did, except the Governor, who arrived home to find them on the floor comfortably hoicking meat out of crab-claws with crochet hooks.

The Governor wasn't angry; if he had been, it would have been easier to forgive him.

Instead, he spoke in a flat voice that rumbled round the room, just as the hillside had vibrated before the explosion.

'Don't ever let me find you eating on the floor like offlanders ever again,' he said.

'I'm sorry,' said Mum, 'I'm sorry. No one saw us. I didn't know it was as bad as that.'

'Of all the people on the colony, why can I not rely on you?' said the Governor. 'Of all the things I have to do, all the people I have to control, all the problems I have to solve, why can I not rely on you?'

And it was true that Mum still sometimes made mistakes when she spoke to the servants; and that sometimes she used words that didn't quite belong where she put them; and that when she was tired her accent became wide and slow, so you could almost bathe in it. But there was no need to make her cry.

Rye was trying to leave the room when the Governor caught hold of his arm.

'Remember you are my son,' he said. 'Everyone else, these offlanders, these workmen, these ignorant people, what they say does not matter, do you understand? Because everything here will be yours one day, and you will be Governor then.'

That evening Rye looked at himself in the mirror.

He found himself wishing that his eyes were not so bright a blue.

29

By morning everything was as if nothing had happened. The Governor filled the house with clanking and puffing and sat down with a hearty appetite for breakfast.

He was really fat, thought Rye, watching the Governor with distaste as he spooned marmalade onto his plate. And his mouth was small and plump and moist. And how could he talk about ignorance, when he didn't even know about the quenchers? If he hadn't destroyed them with his drilling and blasting in the caves.

But then, if the Governor *had* known about them, it wouldn't have stopped him. The Governor wouldn't let any stupid offlander magic get in his way: he wouldn't let anything or anyone get in his way. He would carry on being Governor, carry on being in control of everything, as unstoppable as Clarissa.

In control of everything?

But, of course, he'd never been that, and the fourteen bodies cold in their graves proved it. The Governor had never been the greatest power on the island.

Rye looked across at the Governor and suddenly felt really afraid. There had been another tremor in the night. It had sent everyone stumbling out of doors to wait hollowly for the next one. But this time it hadn't come.

Whose curse had that been, left on the path? Not Harry's, in any case: Harry would have made a better job of it. Kris's? Surely *Kris* would never seek to harm anyone. And what powerful magic was it that had spilled into the crater?

Could the curse have been Stefanie's? She hated everyone: no wonder, when her father was one of the prisoners, just like poor lonely Murray, beaten back into the cave.

But then Stefanie would never have anything to do with offlander magic, Rye was sure of it. Her allegiance was to—what?

'Dad,' said Rye. 'Why is Stefanie's father a prisoner?'

The Governor glared at him.

'That's none of your business, Rye, you know that. Now come along, come along, eat up! Have some marmalade. You've got to be ready for what the day brings. Oils the brain!'

Rye dropped a little marmalade onto his toast; but it sickened him.

Rye flipped through several menus, entered *Arne*, and started a search. With the Comm Station out of action he was going to have to rely on the Governor's confidential files.

He'd known the passwords for a long time.

Arne. Here we were. Right. *Anne*, *Arnold*, *Barnaby* . . . Loads of them. Page down, page down, *Joanne*, *John*.

John. Born . . . school . . . but no, this couldn't be him, this one was a professor.

The entry was a long one. Rye flicked through it. Degree, honours, blah.

One daughter, Stefanie, it said.

Stefanie.

Coincidence?

Rye found himself reading the rest anyway.

Professor John Arne had written a book criticizing the new colonies. It had come out just a few weeks before the big disaster on Colony Three. There had been anti-government protests, and John Arne's picture was on some of the placards. The anti-government movement had grown in size and violence. One of the protesters had a bomb. Someone died.

Rye, interested, pressed Page Down.

Julian Arne, it said. *Film actor of the fifties who became known for his . . .*

What?

Rye checked that he hadn't flicked past anything. But no, that was all there was. Nothing about John Arne for years. What had happened to him?

Rye had another thought and scrolled on through a column of other, more ordinary, Arnes.

Stefanie Arne, it said at last. *Born . . . Daughter of John Arne and Melissa.*

That was the only Stefanie Arne listed. She wasn't listed under Stephanie or Steff, either.

There might be missing entries, though. Perhaps Professor Arne had gone back to being an ordinary scientist, or had died. And Stefanie's father—well, perhaps prisoners' records were kept in another place.

He could ask the girl.

Stefanie.

Stefanie was clever. Rye didn't know how he knew, but he did. She was really clever: thinking, chess-playing clever.

Like a professor's daughter might be.

Rye switched off his screen and twitched the tea towel that was acting as a dust sheet back across the keyboard. There was still dust everywhere: it got past the sheets that Mum and Teresa had hung at the doors and put a metallic taint in everyone's mouth.

Mum caught Rye on the way out. She was still anxious and fussing about yesterday's crab-eating disaster.

'But it was my idea,' pointed out Rye.

'Yes, but I should have known better, shouldn't I?' said Mum, biting at the sides of her nails in the way that annoyed Dad so much. 'I should have known Dad wouldn't like it.'

Rye sighed.

'Is *better* what Dad says it is?' he asked.

Mum blinked and floundered, and pulled at her hair.

'Well, I suppose so,' she said at last. 'Yes, of course it is.'

'So he was right to divert the river and cause the earthquake?'

That confused her even more.

'That was a clever idea, that was, Rye. He wasn't to know it'd turn out—'

'Wrong?'

He thought he'd got her cornered, but Mum's face suddenly cleared. She even smiled.

'Oh, I can't argue with you, Rye,' she said. 'You and your father, you're much too clever for me. I've known that almost from the moment you were born.'

'I know, I know,' said Rye, hastily, before she got started on that again. His mother had gone into labour on board ship, and there had been no doctor or midwife. Dad had delivered Rye with the help of a medical encyclopedia, carefully following all the diagrams and pointing out where Mum was going wrong.

The story got more dramatic and important every time it was told: but it always ended the same way.

'Oh, but you were the bonniest baby, Rye, love. All the ship drank your health, and the captain gave you a cuttlefish he'd brought for his parrot for you to chew on, and the purser said it was sure to make you a good talker.'

Rye went out and down the road leaving a trail of red footprints behind him in the damp dust.

He needed to see Kris. To talk about offlander things. Offlander magic. Keeping things safe. If he sat on the doorstep long enough then someone must come out. And then, perhaps, he would call in at the Hostel on his way back home. Talk to Stefanie. Find out about her dad.

Perhaps.

30

The Shoremans' metal-box house stood on the hillside apart from the others. You came upon it quite suddenly: you hauled your way up the track, over a bump, and there it was in front of you.

And today there was someone sitting outside in a chair made from an old oil drum. Rye felt a rush of gladness.

'Lisa!'

She looked up, smiled, tried to say something, but only succeeded in bringing on a fit of coughing.

Harry Shoreman came out of the house with a cup of something. Rye couldn't help staring at him, because he'd shaved off his magnificent moustaches, and now Rye could see that his upper lip, like his chest, was covered in intricate blue swirls.

'Lisa not talk,' he said. 'All cough, cough. Not well.'

'I'm sorry,' said Rye, forcing his eyes away from Harry's lip. 'I'm very sorry. Is that—is that magic stuff you're giving Lisa?'

Harry shrugged.

'What magic? Tell me that, first, then I tell you.'

Rye was silenced.

'Look,' said Harry Shoreman, getting a thing like a fat cigar from his pocket. 'This leaf of stinkwort, yes? And inside bullrush. And other things. Watch!'

He placed it on the ground, struck a match on his shoe, and brought it over to the leaf-bundle. The thing caught at once, spitting and flaring, until the flame blazed into a steady squint-white.

And then, with a soft *woomph*, the thing spread out into a giant flower shape, and suddenly the whole place smelt nose-scouringly of mothballs and boot polish.

Lisa and Rye coughed until their eyes streamed.

'Will that stuff really make Lisa better?' spluttered Rye at last, wiping his smarting eyes.

Harry looked at him steadily.

'It help Lisa breathe. But Lisa want strength, yes? That somewhere else.'

'Where?'

'Somewhere else,' said Harry, again, rather shortly. 'She find it. *I* find it, when time right. I find much strength for her, and for the other ill ones.'

'By magic?' asked Rye; but someone came round the corner from the back of the house before Harry could answer.

It was Kris. He stopped short, close-faced, when he saw Rye.

'I didn't know you were here,' he said; but someone else was following him round the corner and stopping short too.

It was the girl.

The three of them stood and stared at each other, and Rye wanted to say, *What is she doing here?*

'These two, they work,' said Harry Shoreman.

Rye relaxed slightly at that. Of course. Lisa was ill, so they'd needed someone to clean the floors and peel the vegetables. That was all right.

'Every day, Stefanie help. She good girl.'

Rye felt anger rising within himself again at the thought of the girl in the house every day, when the door had been closed to him.

But then he was the Governor's son, and they were offlanders. They could hardly have asked him to help nurse Lisa.

126

So it was still all right.

'They clean barn,' went on Harry Shoreman. 'Lisa, she cough, she cough: no one sleep. Now we take turns sleep in barn. It nice, now. You go, you go see.'

But the girl was sending a warning glance to Kris; and at that Rye caught his anger and held onto it.

He shouldered his way past them and made his way round the house.

The barn was really no more than a hut made of rocks and mud, with a roof of old pallets and fern, and a bit of perspex wedged in for a window.

They'd put a new floor in; that was the first thing he noticed. Instead of bare earth there were duckboards. And there were big fern-stuffed cushions, too: woolly, comfortable jumper-grey and jumper-blue.

His anger surged higher.

And there—over in the corner—books. Half a dozen of them. And on top an exercise book.

Rye picked it up.

aaaaaaaaaaaaaaaaa
bbbbbbbbbbbbbbbbbb
ggggggggggggggggg

and on, and on, in awkward pencil.

The hut was suddenly too small for Rye. It could not contain the anger that was rushing out of him and scorching all the oxygen in the place to cinders.

Kris was just outside the door.

'Stefanie's been showing me how to read and write,' he said, awkwardly, as if he were admitting something.

Rye snorted.

'It won't be any good. You're an offlander, you won't be able to.'

'Oh yes he can.'

Stefanie stepped up behind Kris and faced Rye squarely.

127

'It was hard for him, because offlanders travel round things all the time in their minds. But now he understands what he has to do, he can read.'

Rye thought of Stefanie and Kris together in the barn while he had trudged up the hill, and knocked at the house, and gone away lonely.

He spoke viciously.

'You can't be a proper offlander if you can read,' he said.

'No,' said Kris. 'No, I can't.'

Rye could feel his rage flying out until it was stretching him in all directions. But there was nothing for it to hit, so it carried on outwards, until he was suddenly terribly afraid that he was going to snap and break.

He would go away at once and find someone to spend his rage on: Mum, or Charlie Box, or Robin Willis.

He turned away from the hut; but as he did his reflection in the warped perspex window caught his eye. And in it he looked older, fatter, darker.

And an even bigger fear raced upon him, stooped upon him like a hungry frigate-bird, and hit him with such force that it knocked everything else away.

Rye's rage fell around him and shattered like shards of glass. He hardly dared move, surrounded as he was by them.

Rye looked from Stefanie to Kris. He suddenly wanted their help, though he wasn't sure with what.

'It's not my fault that Dad's the Governor,' he said.

But Stefanie's face was like stone.

'The Governor is keeping my father prisoner,' she said, 'even though he's never done anything except study things, and try to make sure that good things aren't destroyed. The Governor's wrecking the island, and Kris's heritage with it. He almost killed Kris's mother.'

And half of Rye wanted to lash out at her, bash her out of the way, snap, *Nonsense!*

'But he's not Rye,' said Kris, suddenly.

'Isn't he? What's the difference?'

Rye felt the dark fear again, but he resisted it fiercely.

'The Governor wants to make this place a . . . a monument to human happiness,' he said.

Stefanie actually laughed.

'Even the gods didn't do a very good job of that,' she said.

31

R ye typed in *Makepeace* and started a search. There
weren't that many Makepeaces. There was an
Arthur, and a Cuthbert, and a Maria.

Here it was.

Ryland Makepeace.

It was quite a long entry, though not as long as John
Arne's had been. Birth, school, university. Rye had never
really wondered about it. Dad didn't talk about himself
much. He talked about ideas, things to do. But not about
himself.

Dad had got a Government job. Something to do with
farm animals.

Yes, Rye had known that, sort of. He remembered the
pigs Dad had taken him to see years ago when they were
on the mainland, and the pentagon crabs. Dad always
wanted all the animals to be big and fat and the same.
Yes, here it was. Some sort of special breeding programme
. . . and a medal, a gold medal, for finding a way to
reproduce animals all exactly the same.

A gold medal. That was really something. Really
something to be proud of. His dad, with a gold medal.

Ryland Makepeace had been a member of the team sent
out to Colony Three. Ground-breaking blah blah blah.
Promising signs of success; but the end of the project
resulted in his return to the mainland.

Then it went on to the rest of Dad's career, but that
was annoying because it didn't tell you why Colony Three
had come to an end. Anyway, the rest of the entry was just

more blah, stuff he knew. Rye ignored it and typed in *Colony Three*.

There wasn't much. It had been the first colony to be set up on one of the Oceanic Islands. Within three years the population had numbered over two hundred.

That wasn't many: smaller than this colony, if you counted the prisoners. So what had gone wrong?

The first sign of a serious problem had been when some of the farm animals were born with abnormalities. At first a fault in cloning techniques had been suspected; but an investigation had cleared staff of any negligence.

That included Dad, probably: a younger Dad; a less fat Dad. Rye screwed up his face, but it was hard to imagine Dad's being young—as young as Robin Willis. Surely Dad had always been like a small but important volcano, emitting bursts of enthusiasm and anger as he went along.

Rye wondered what Mum's job had been on the colony. She might have been a cook, perhaps, or someone who cleaned out the animals.

A *very* odd couple.

He read the last paragraph.

Radiation pollution was discovered, but before a survey could be conducted an explosion took place which resulted in the death of about half the population of the colony. The cause was never fully explained, but protesters against the development of the island were possibly involved. A large part of the settlement was affected, and all the survivors were found to have been rendered sterile by long-term exposure to the background radiation that had affected cloning procedures. The island was evacuated immediately and the project closed.

Rye sat and stared at his keyboard. Another colony, another disaster. Dimly, he could understand that might bring two people together. Being so near to death would fill

131

you with the desire to live, live, get as much out of life as you possibly could.

Mum had been Cinderella. That was what she had always said. Dad had been the bright young man in charge of a whole project, and she'd just been . . . someone ordinary.

'Things weren't easy,' she'd said. 'But he worked so hard. He wanted so much for it all to work.'

All the girls on the colony had had an eye on him. He was the handsomest man in the place.

Handsome? The fat man with the brisk cheerfulness that blatted aside everything in its path?

And then in the end the handsome prince had gone to the humble adoring frog-type person and asked her . . .

And they had lived happily ever after.

Rye shifted in his chair. There was something wrong with this. He flicked back up through the article and read it again.

Then he found what it was. A wash of cold swept right through him, as if a wave had broken out of the computer screen and drenched him. He sat for a minute, trying to imagine a way out of the tangle; and then he went to the dictionary and looked up *sterile*.

That was what he'd thought: *unable to produce offspring*.

The year before he was born, his parents had been exposed to radiation for so long that it had made them unable to have children.

He ran it through his mind several times, trying to settle it into some sort of sense. But it wouldn't go.

The year before—

It was like being born again.

Rye felt as if he'd been at the bottom of a great lake; he'd been living deep, deep in the mud, but now he was floating upwards towards the light.

32

The world had changed so utterly that Rye had to keep touching things to make sure they were still real. He ran his hand down the door to feel the lustrous paint, and, underneath it, just faintly, the grain of the wood.

Mum was sitting in the dining room. The table was spread for tea, all properly, with the little bowls and trinkety things to make it civilized; and there wasn't a sign that she'd survived one world's end and was in the middle—middle? beginning?—of another.

The Governor wasn't there, but since the 'quake he seldom was.

Mum smiled at Rye just as if—just as if she was his mum.

Rye felt everything shift again to the new world he had only just discovered. Habit made him keep falling back to the old one, and he had to keep up a constant vigilance against that happening. So: this was not Mum.

Who was it, then?

Maria Makepeace. A woman who had looked after him since before he could remember. Who had served him and adored him.

It was odd, but it almost made her seem more important than before.

'I had Teresa make some layer cake,' said Mum. 'I don't think we've had one since we've been here. Do you remember, we always used to have layer cake on holidays?'

Rye did remember: except that the people he remembered were not real. Had never been real. Rye and his mum and dad.

Not real.

Remember. Always remember.

Mum—not Mum, but—oh, whoever it was—was chatting on.

'We always used to have them when I was a girl,' she said. 'My mother, she wasn't one for novelty, so it was always layer cake. I remember we used to tease her about it, until one day she got niggled and picked it up and put it down on its side and said, *There you are: blessed full-moon cake*. Oh, we did laugh.'

'Is that true?' asked Rye, bluntly. He'd heard the story many times before; but now nothing was to be trusted.

Mum—the person who had always been Mum—blinked at him.

'Well, of course it is,' she said. 'I haven't got much of a talent for making up stories, Rye: I just keep trotting out the old ones.'

Of course she did: because Dad could rehearse all the inconsistencies out of them. Try them out on someone too young to know any better, so they became part of him; part of who he was.

Large parts of himself were unreal. That was what this all meant. Rye looked down at himself and almost expected to see holes all the way through, like a mountain cheese.

Mum—Maria—picked up a knife and began to saw carefully at the cake.

'No, I was never much good at stories,' she said. 'I always liked to hear them, mind. My sister, she was the one: she'd tell you ghost stories that'd stand your hair on end, she would. And then we'd all scream, and stepdad'd come in, and then we'd be for it!' She smiled a little sadly.

134

Rye had never met any of her family; he'd always supposed they were dead.

But then he'd always supposed all sorts of things.

'And Dad, of course; he'd make you roar. When he was young you could hardly get near him because all the girls in the place would shimmy round. We got into trouble, sometimes, for ignoring the other men.'

That sounded true. But then it all sounded true. Rye would have said that she was too stupid to tell lies, except for the one story she did tell, again and again and again, about being on a ship with no doctor or midwife and the captain giving her baby a cuttlefish to chew and—and on, and on, and *it wasn't true*.

He raised his eyes and looked at her. Her honey-coloured hair was coiled into wayward tendrils, as it always was in this damp climate. Her face was soft and pink. She got out of breath easily. She could just about read and write.

And she loved him deeply.

'When I was born—'

'Oh, Rye, yes! I was so frightened that things would go wrong. And there was Dad with his nose in a book telling me my pains weren't coming fast enough. Well, they were coming fast enough for me, I can tell you!'

Rye felt as if he was flickering between one world and the other: between what-was-true and what-is-true. Because in his heart it *was* true: but it was still impossible.

'I don't believe it,' he said.

She stopped gabbling and stared at him; but she was used to not understanding.

'How can you have given birth to me,' he went on, carefully, relentlessly, 'when you and Dad had been living on Colony Three. How could you have children after that?'

She sat, frozen, with her mouth open.

135

'How did you—?'

He shrugged.

'I looked it up on the computer.'

Rye might as well have said he'd found it in Holy Writ. She didn't understand computers well enough to know that they could tell lies, too.

She ran her hands through her hair, and more of it escaped to make a soft haze round her head.

'It *is* true,' she said, a little defiantly. 'I've not been lying to you, Rye. I wouldn't never have done that.'

He turned his blue eyes on her and she quailed a little.

'But how can it be true?' he demanded.

Mum got up and her napkin fell to the floor unheeded. Dad had trained her to use her napkin, but she'd always forgotten it by the end of the meal.

She held out her hand.

'You come with me and I'll show you,' she said.

33

'I don't understand it, mind,' she said, as she opened the door to her bedroom, 'but I expect it'll all be as clear as day to you. You're clever, like Dad. It must be a fine thing to be clever,' she finished up, a little wistfully.

She reached up on to the top shelf of one of the heavy wardrobes that lined her bedroom and brought out a little wooden box. She sat down on the bed and opened it to reveal a lining of cheap shiny scarlet. She started to sort through the chains and pendants and brooches that were tangled inside.

'This is all stuff from before I was married,' she said, stopping just for an instant to admire a tarnished heart-shaped earring. 'I couldn't wear any of it now, of course, it's not ladylike enough; but it reminds me of those days. And Dad would never look through this. Here we are.'

Her fingers nipped in among the jumble and picked out something small. She put it in Rye's outstretched hand.

'There,' she said.

It was a capsule, the sort of thing the doctor might give you, red at one end and clear at the other. In tiny writing on the red bit there were some numbers and a few letters: an abbreviation of a scientific name.

Rye stared at it blankly.

'What is it?'

'It's what Dad gave me,' said Mum, earnestly. 'A whole load I had to take, at just the right times. Dad gave me an extra one in case I dropped one down a crack in the floorboards, or something, but I was ever so careful. So I kept that one, just in case something went wrong, and then it might help the doctor.'

Rye hadn't a clue what she was talking about.

'Help the doctor with what?'

'You, of course.'

Mum was so used to people knowing more than she did that she never understood how much she had to tell.

'But . . . what were the tablets for?'

'Well, for the animals, really. That's what they were supposed to be for, anyway, but Dad, he assured me that he'd sorted them out so it would be all right. So I could carry you, even though I couldn't have children of my own any more. *It won't turn me into a pig, will it?* I said; and that made him laugh. Oh, and I did so want him to love me. So I trusted him, and of course it was all right. We even got married, and everything—I didn't have anything special to wear, which was a pity, but then it couldn't be helped, could it?—right there among all the wreckage. And then Dad took me to the Animal Centre. All the other people from there had been evacuated, so we had the place to ourselves. Dad gave me an injection to put me to sleep. I was frightened about that, but he told me that when I woke up I'd be carrying a baby. *A boy,* he said. *Just exactly like me.*'

Rye remembered the pigs so long ago on the mainland. They had all been exactly the same; and so had the pentagon crabs Dad had had brought in. That was what Dad's job had been, making things that were the same.

At first a fault in cloning techniques had been suspected.

The room moved a quarter-turn round him and then turned black-and-white. He sat down suddenly on the bed, and the bounce made Mum's little box fall over and spill gaudy junk across the bedspread. Rye rested his elbows on his knees and breathed slowly and deeply until the bedspread had flushed back to glossy purple.

Mum was talking, talking. Mostly the Governor had trained her to keep quiet, but sometimes when she was excited she forgot.

'Dad made sure we were off the mainland when you were born,' she said. 'He didn't want any doctors to see you, you see. Because the way you came—well, it had to be secret because it wasn't allowed. Dad, he made you come a bit early so people would think you were begun before the accident. And he made me promise never to tell anyone. He told me that again and again, never never to tell anyone.'

'He was right,' said Rye, and his voice croaked as he said it. 'You should never have told anyone.'

Mum twisted her hands together, and her mouth went twisted, too, with doubt.

'But you thought I'd lied to you,' she said. 'And I never have. Never. I gave birth to you and fed you. So that must make me your mum, mustn't it?'

'I don't know,' said Rye, dully.

'And you wouldn't want to be like me,' she went on, eagerly. 'I'm not clever. I don't know things like you and Dad do. And you couldn't find a better man than Dad, could you? No one wanted to give him a job after Colony Three failed, not even though it wasn't his fault at all, not a bit. But he worked himself up again, and now he's Governor.'

And I am him, thought Rye, suddenly so cold. Exactly the same. I'll be fat, and my voice will rumble, and I'll get into rages, and everyone will be afraid of me.

He looked at his hands. His fingers had square ends. His thumbs curved backwards. His nails were neat and pink and never needed cutting.

And they belonged to someone else.

139

34

Rye walked. He walked as fast as he could, to try to stop himself thinking. He walked up the track as fast as he could go until he had a stitch in his side and he was panting.

Hwoof, hwoof, he gasped.

Just like the Governor on his exercise machine.

Rye stopped. The mudflats were gleaming dully all the way out to the faraway silver line that marked the sea.

And there was the Governor now, below him, walking with prim little steps from the new prison entrance down to the Comm Station. There was a blustery wind that kept blowing up the bottom of his tie. He stopped to tuck it into his trousers, and Rye wanted to scream. Rye turned away from the settlement and began walking again. Perhaps if he walked fast enough and far enough he would escape— walk out of his skin like a salamander—come out all fresh and gleaming.

And the same.

He was high above the settlement, now. Beneath him was Harry Shoreman's food stall. The group of men round it must mean that it was open again. Lisa must be able to look after herself a bit more.

No, there was Kris.

There was Kris, cooking fish cakes and onions.

Just like his dad.

Just like his dad.

Oh, and Kris wasn't even all Harry's: Kris had Lisa's

smile, Lisa's chin; and still he was frying burgers on his dad's food stall.

And there, there, far below him, was the little figure of Stefanie, pegging out washing on the Hostel line.

Rye could have wept with the waste of it. They were all chained down. Every child was where it was, what it was, because of its parents; not one ever got the chance to start afresh, to be itself. By the time it could be free of its parents it was warped, spoiled, corrupted, by a million examples, and a million orders, and a thousand bits of attention and neglect and reward and punishment.

And how could you shake away all that?

Rye stood at the top of the hill and the wind blew around him. He held his arms away from his sides and imagined the Governor part of him peeling off like a sloughed skin and being whipped away, far away, into the secret middle of the island where no one ever came. He imagined one of the great salamanders stalking it and tearing it to slow shreds with its little teeth.

Gone.

Rye drew a deep breath.

Now he was a new person.

A new person, fresh-minted.

What was the new person going to do?

'Hey, Rye!' called Gabriel, over Clarissa's genteel phuttering. 'Want to take charge for a while?'

'Thank you very much indeed,' said Rye, politely, 'but I don't want to hold you up. I expect you're anxious to finish off and get down to the Hostel.'

Gabriel turned to give him a quizzical look.

'Well, I'm not that desperate,' he said. 'You can come on up if you like.'

'Oh no, I don't want to make more work for you. I just

came down to make sure everything was all right. I hope you get finished soon, Gabriel. Give my best wishes to Annie when you see her. Goodbye.'

Rye clambered back up to the track. A voice called after him.

'Hey, Rye!' it said. 'Are you *feeling* all right?'

The Governor got home very late. His shoes were plastered in white mud. They had finally managed to trace the new course the river had worn away for itself.

'I'll need every man from daybreak,' he said. 'Rye, go and post up the notices Miss Last gives you: one at the Hostel, and another at the crossroads.'

'Is it really serious?' asked Rye.

'Yes.'

No one needed to have the danger spelled out to them: with every minute the water was washing away more and more of that soft layer of rock, and the hills were pressing down ever more heavily on what was left. The men turned up with spades and pickaxes and they worked. Even Harry Shoreman came. Rye did what he could to help, but it was frustrating because they kept having to stop so that the engineers could lay explosives; and then there was the wait for the roll-call before anything could be detonated. The Governor paced backwards and forwards. When the work was brought to a halt for ten minutes because young Kevin Frost went to answer a call of nature without telling anyone, the volcanic attack the Governor launched on Kevin reduced him very nearly to tears.

I'd never shout like that, thought Rye: I'd never lose my temper as badly as that with anyone.

'Rye!'

Gabriel's giant frame was covered in splashes of red and white.

'Look, take over Clarissa, will you? They need someone with muscle over there.'

Working Clarissa was easy, except that Rye's visibility was reduced by the mud spattered on the cabin walls. He'd have to invent a cleaning system—washers, or wipers—but for now, Rye scooped and spun and deposited tons of slimy earth in Hercules's dumper truck. The worst moment was when he was slewing and reversing simultaneously and he nearly knocked Marty into his next life with Clarissa's boom. By the time Rye had finished bawling at Marty for being stupid enough to get in the way, Marty had slunk off and was apparently trying to dig himself a faraway grave in the mud.

Rye, seething, went back to work. He tried not to notice how many people were grinning behind his back.

And then something happened. It was quite sudden, and for a few moments Rye thought that Clarissa had developed a fault. Her joysticks, that always moved so sweetly and easily, suddenly went heavy and stiff under his hands.

He turned in the cabin to call over to Gabriel; but turning was suddenly a slow, hauling effort, as if his bones had turned to lead.

I must be ill, he thought—but all around him everyone else had gone into slow motion, too. Men were dragging the heads of their pickaxes as they lifted them, and people were leaning over their spades, suddenly short of breath.

Only Harry Shoreman seemed unaffected.

The Governor snapped everybody back to work again, but they hardly had strength to move. They staggered on for another ten minutes until there was a pause for a charge to be laid. Then they all threw themselves down in the mud and sat with their heads in their hands until the explosion, which woke most of them up.

Gabriel wiped the sweat off his forehead.

143

'I feel like a sick kitten,' he said, chest heaving and bewildered. 'What's happening, Rye?'

The Governor stumbled past, snapping *Come along, come along, we'll be there soon!* but his face was red and his eyes full of baffled anger.

What was happening?

The Governor heaved Dicky Paton to his feet with an impatient hand, but Dicky only stumbled half a dozen steps before he went down again.

What was happening?

'I feel like something's taken all my strength away,' breathed Gabriel; and there was something like fear in his eyes.

Strength? Who had talked about strength? About finding it, or losing it?

Lisa want strength, yes?

Harry Shoreman.

I find it. I find it when time right.

Oh great gods! thought Rye, remembering the red bundle containing the moon-flower that had fallen into the crater. How much strength would Harry's magic take?

The Governor was dragging Dicky to his feet again, and chasing him back to work, and standing over him while he did it.

I'd never do that, thought Rye, though all the time he was conscious of the water underground which was washing away the soft rock on which the hills stood.

Harry Shoreman went over and worked beside Dicky, giving him what help he could. Everyone else put their heads down and got on with it. But it was hard, hard work, when even their hands felt heavy.

After Dicky collapsed for the third time, the Governor seized Dicky's spade and began to dig himself. He was ham-fisted, ungainly, inept, and his jacket flapped stupidly behind him: but no one laughed. They didn't have the energy, for one thing; but that was not the only reason they didn't laugh.

The men worked on, doggedly, lifting tools again and again that were three times as heavy as they should be. And they would have given up straight away, except for the double threat of the water underground and of the Governor beside them.

And now, thank heavens, thank heavens, the engineers were calling another halt: but no one could rest, yet, for they were ordered to take their tools and move up the slope. And Rye had to walk with them, because Gabriel was taking over Clarissa and carrying Dicky in her up to the brow of the hill.

They waited for the engineers to detonate the explosive. The noise was dull, but then its echo came to meet it, and the echo of the echo, all merged into long thunder.

And suddenly, like a miracle, the earth was spewing out a great spout of water. It fell raggedly at first, until it found its way, but then it gathered speed and volume and rushed joyfully down the gully they had dug, round the outcrop of tougher rock that had resisted even the dynamite of the engineers, and home into its old channel that led to the sea.

And almost at that moment the great weight that had oppressed them all dissolved, and all their strength returned.

And the joy of the tumbling water entered into them, and they cheered.

Rye must have got home just after Robin Willis, for he was in the cloakroom easing his feet out of his shoes: from the squashed shape of his feet they were, like his suit, at least a size and a half too small.

145

'How was your day, Robin?' asked Rye, still triumphant.

'Very tiring, I'm afraid,' he answered, bravely.

Tiring? When all he'd been doing was fiddling about with the Comm Station? Rye found himself tapping his fingers impatiently on the seam of his trousers: but that was one of the Governor's mannerisms, so he folded his arms. The Governor was too fat to fold his arms comfortably.

'I'm afraid that it's giving you ever such a lot of trouble,' he said, hauling up all the sweet concern he could. 'Do let me know if there is anything I can do to help.'

Rye went out, leaned against the door frame, and took in a deep breath. That hadn't been anything like the Governor. It hadn't.

The effort had nearly killed him, but it *hadn't* been like the Governor.

Robin Willis's wet-seaweedy head popped suddenly out of the door beside him.

'Are you feeling *well*?' he asked.

35

C ompletely new person day.

Bath, not shower, no slippers. Hair parted on the side with all the bounce wetted down. T-shirt, oldest trousers.

Practise smiling in new way that involves showing bottom teeth.

Breakfast: bread, yeast spread but no butter. Also tea without sugar.

'Are you all right, Rye?' asked Mum, really anxious.

Rye tried to summon up the energy to be nice to her; but it was too embarrassing.

'I just felt like a change,' he muttered.

When Rye got up from the table he let his napkin drop down onto the floor like Dad never did.

He felt slightly, annoyingly, guilty about that for the rest of the day.

He went to his room and arranged all his books in non-alphabetical order. He wanted them random, but that was difficult because he kept spotting patterns. In the end he spent an hour writing a computer program to do it for him.

The books looked an irritating mess when he'd finished; but he left them, even the big encyclopedia that overhung the shelf the computer had assigned it, and went out.

Every time he met someone he smiled his new smile that showed his bottom teeth. Nearly everyone was too startled to smile back; but Marty, who by some miracle

147

happened to be upright two mornings running, beamed back a yellow grin and tipped his cap.

'That's the ticket,' he said. 'Nice and cheery, young fellow. Growing up just like your dad, ain't ya?'

Which halted Rye in his tracks.

Cheery?

Yes, dammit, of course the Governor was cheery. The Governor pranced along with his chins wobbling, beaming and shaking hands and enquiring after everybody.

Rye went and found a rock to sit on, and had a radical re-think.

Gloom and misery. That was the thing; and it would be much easier.

Gloom.

Rye heaved himself wearily to his feet and dragged them up to the food stall. Kris was raking out the burners. He took one look at Rye and said:

'Are you all right?'

Which was what everyone was asking.

Rye heaved up a sigh.

'I'm fine,' he said, bravely.

'Oh. Good.'

There was a pause.

'Mum's ever such a lot better,' said Kris. 'We're going to leave her by herself this afternoon. So if you were free— there's a place I could show you, if you like.'

'Where is it?'

Kris carried on raking the cinders.

'It's a secret,' he said, his cheeks a bit red.

'Oh. Does Stefanie know about it?'

But Kris only grinned.

'She wouldn't be interested,' he said. 'Anyway, she's got that great cut on her arm, so she can't do much.'

'Clumsy idiot,' said Rye. 'She did it on a shell, somehow. Heaven knows how.'

Kris gave him a very straight glance.

'Mm,' he said. 'It's hard to imagine how it could have happened.'

But Rye wasn't all that interested in Stefanie.

'So . . . is it . . . is it an offlander place?' he asked.

Kris looked at him hard again, and this time it was Rye's turn to flush.

'It's a private secret,' Kris said.

Rye was flattered, and rather touched.

'I promise I won't tell,' he said.

'I know you won't,' said Kris.

'Do you? How?'

A couple of men in warders' uniforms were coming up the path looking for a mid-morning snack.

'Because if our dads found out about it they'd half kill us,' said Kris. 'See you back here after the lunchtime rush, OK? Morning, Mr Bruce; morning, Mr Finn. What can I do for you?'

Kris led Rye over the hill and down towards the beach. They saw a salamander on the way, a real giant, five feet long and smelling of acid. It was trying to swallow a snake. The snake was wriggling fiercely when they first saw it, but gradually its movements became feebler until it hung as limply as a bootlace from the salamander's smug jaws.

'It was worth coming for that,' said Rye, forgetting for a moment about being gloomy. 'There's always something brilliant to see on the island, Kris.'

'It's just down this way,' said Kris.

There was a narrow gully that led crookedly down to the sea. And behind a joined-on outcrop of rock there was a bit of rubbish that had been pushed behind a giant clump of fern.

'Wow,' said Rye, suddenly realizing what it was. 'It's brilliant. How did you get it here?'

'I floated it round. I made it and got it here all in a night. I couldn't sleep for Mum's coughing, so I went for a walk, and there was a whole load of stuff dumped by the warehouse. There was even the rope to tie the drums on.'

'And does it really float? Even with you on it?'

'Help me get it down to the water and I'll show you.'

The raft was only a couple of pallets with oil drums tied to it, but it floated like a dream. In fact, the oil drums worked so well that the raft was actually a catamaran; which was stylish, but made it so precarious that the whole thing tipped up at the slightest provocation.

'If we let some water into the drums it'd make it more stable,' said Rye.

'It would do,' agreed Kris. 'Except that then she'd be harder to dock. Anyway, falling in's the best bit.'

Kris had a point; and the air was nearly always so damp here that your clothes were hardly ever properly dry, anyway.

'We can fish from it,' said Rye. 'Look, I've got some string. We can bait it with pea crabs. Bet I catch an ivory shark. Do your shark-chant, Kris, to call one up.'

'An ivory shark would break the string.'

'Or drag me to a bloody anguished death. Give me a hand, Kris.'

They perched on the raft and let it float in aimless circles, being always careful not to let it go anywhere near the main channel where they might be taken by the tide or spotted from the settlement.

'My dad would go berserk if he knew where I was,' said Rye, lying blissfully on his stomach and peering into the water.

'So would mine,' said Kris; and they grinned at each other.

150

'But isn't this a really offlander thing to do?' asked Rye, after a pause. 'You know, sailing and rafts?'

'Well . . . not oil drum rafts,' said Kris.

'No, this is a super-modern hi-tech raft, obviously,' agreed Rye. And then he said: 'What were the boats made of, Kris? You know, before?'

'Tree trunks. Sort of hollowed out.'

'Oh. But . . . there aren't any trees on the island, Kris.'

'No,' said Kris. 'There aren't, now.'

And Rye remembered the layer of charcoal ash in the grave around the skulls. He was silent for a time.

'Your dad's shaved off his moustache,' he said, at last. 'I didn't know he was tattooed like that. Is that an offlander thing?'

'Yes. Well . . . it's a magic thing. We were doing some stuff to help Mum.'

'Yes,' said Rye, remembering the suffocating weight that had fallen on them all the day before. 'I know. How do they do the tattoos?'

They were lying gazing into the sea, and somehow talking was easy.

'With a piece of human bone. It's filed into points. They dip it into stuff made from burnt soapweed and then hammer it into the skin.'

Rye nearly said *Does it hurt?* but it was just too stupid a question to ask.

'Will you have it done, Kris? On your face?'

Kris took quite a long time to reply.

'Mum's not keen,' he said. 'It makes you ill, for one thing. But it's part of being an offlander. One of the parts . . . Dad's teaching me loads of stuff, Rye. Songs and prayers and rituals. Some of it's incredible. I mean, really useful.'

'Are there ways of protecting the island?' asked Rye. 'Protecting the island from . . . from people?'

Kris hesitated.

151

'That's not the sort of stuff offlanders do, really. We're better at hunting than protecting. We've done what we can, but even Dad doesn't think it'll do all that much good.' He stopped for a moment, and then went on: 'You know, I'm not sure magic ever does any good.'

'But Lisa's better?'

'Yes. Much. Quite suddenly, yesterday afternoon. But I'm not sure that was magic.'

'Oh, I am,' said Rye, with a shiver. 'Quite, quite sure.'

There was a pause, and then Kris went on, slowly:

'There was another bit of magic. Something I did by myself. It was after the earthquake, when I thought Mum wasn't going to get better. I was so angry that . . . that I did something to the Governor. But I don't think it can have worked. And now . . . now I'm glad it didn't.'

So it had been Kris.

Rye thought of the grave that Clarissa had dug, and about Murray, lonely on the hillside, and found that there was no anger towards Kris inside himself.

'Show me how to do some magic,' he said. 'Just one thing. Please. I still say that prayer to Aranui.'

But Kris shook his head.

'No. Dad wouldn't want me to. Anyway, it's offlander stuff: *our* power. Your people have got enough of your own . . . except there's lots to learn, Rye, and only me to learn it. I mean, I wouldn't have *time* to go to school. But—I don't know—I thought that perhaps if it was written down . . . '

'I know what it's like,' said Rye, suddenly. 'Having to carry things on.'

'Yes,' said Kris. 'I thought you would.'

They floated round in circles and nothing took the bait.

'We'll try the other side of the cove next time,' said Rye, at last. 'Hey, look, I've got something. Wow, look at this! A crab the size of a giant man-eating hair-louse. Look at the claws on it!'

Kris glanced over; and then he peered at the tiny thing more closely.

'It's got its claws the wrong way round,' he said.

Rye blinked at it.

'Perhaps it's left-handed,' he said. 'Like you.'

'Never seen a left-handed one before.'

Neither had Rye, now he came to think about it.

'A new species?' he suggested.

Kris glanced at him sideways, and was silent. When he did speak, it was in a voice that echoed flatly and falsely off the water.

'When was the last time you saw a crab carrying eggs, Rye?'

Rye stared.

'I don't know. Ages ago. I suppose this isn't the season for it.'

'This was the season for it last year.'

Rye opened his mouth to argue, but then hesitated. As far as Rye could remember, Kris was right. Last year at this time the shore had been populated by aggressive egg-bearing crabs going menacingly about like miniature tanks. Rye remembered the excitement of finding the first one; and later the incessant keening of the gorging gulls; and how bored he was with them by the end of the breeding season.

'Perhaps they only breed every other year,' said Rye. 'Or perhaps it's to do with the moon, not the time of year.'

But even as he said it, he knew it wasn't true. Something was stopping the crabs from breeding. Rye tried to shove the problem to the back of his mind, but all that did was jostle the problems that were already there.

The crabs he'd eaten with Mum had been poor empty things. And their mouth feelers had been green and soft.

153

What was happening to them?

Perhaps he should mention it to the Governor.

But there he was again, back at the Governor. The Governor followed Rye around, as impossible to escape as a shadow, but much, much heavier.

And here was Rye, fishing happily and busily, when he had meant to spend a gloomy day.

Rye shook his head impatiently and chucked the odd-clawed little crab back into the sea.

It floated for just long enough for him to be almost sure it had died.

36

That evening Rye went for a walk on the shore. He wanted to be alone, to think, and so, of course, the first thing he did was fall over Stefanie, who was crouched down by the culvert that handled the overflow from the prison. She was fishing, too, but instead of a bucket beside her she had a set of kitchen scales.

'I'm weighing them,' she said, scowling.

'What?'

'You heard.'

She pulled on the line and a flat-crab appeared, clinging greedily to the bait. Stefanie waited tensely, grabbed, and flipped it upside down in the scoop of the scales. Rye hung around, intrigued.

'The crabs are really light at the moment,' he said.

'Yes,' said Stefanie, making a note in an exercise book. 'It's the plague.'

'What?' said Rye, again, startled.

'The plague. Your precious father introduced it with his precious pentagon crabs that no one's allowed to catch. It stops the flat-crabs digesting their food properly, and so they starve to death. It affects other animals, too.'

Well, that was rubbish. At least, Rye sort of thought it was. But he remembered the little odd-shaped crab he'd thrown back into the water.

'The Governor wouldn't introduce animals that were diseased,' he said.

'They weren't diseased,' said Stefanie, speaking loudly and slowly, as though he were stupid: 'but they were carrying the plague virus. It'll wipe out most of the life in the sea over the next year or two. It's happened on just about every other colony that's been established. They had to abandon Colony Two altogether because the plague killed all the local rats and they poisoned the water supply.'

'But that would never happen,' said Rye, trying not to think about it too much. 'You've got it all wrong. All that stuff's been worked out really properly by experts.'

Stefanie made a harsh sound that was a little like laughter.

'Experts in what?'

'Anyway,' said Rye, swiftly, 'the pentagon crabs are doing all right, aren't they? So it just means that they'll take over. And the pentagon crabs are all really big, and so—'

'Yes, isn't it brilliant,' said Stefanie, scathingly. 'Lots of big juicy fat crabs: and what do they eat? Why, dead things, of course. So at the moment they're bursting, aren't they, because the sea is lousy with dying sealife. But what are they going to eat next year, when everything else has rotted down to slime? Although I don't suppose that'll make much difference, because those pentagon crabs are all clones, and clones have a habit of dropping dead before they are old enough to mate, anyway.'

Stefanie pulled in another flat-crab, weighed it, marked its shell with a pen, and threw it down-current. Then she glanced back at Rye.

'Are you all right?' she asked.

Rye, who was having another black-and-white phase, decided to sit down.

'You *are* all right, aren't you?' persisted Stefanie. 'Because I didn't mean—'

'I'm fine, I'm fine.' He glared at her. 'You just don't know what you're talking about, that's all.'

156

'Yes I do. My father is a scientist, and—'

'Well, so is mine!' broke in Rye, in sudden anger.

Always the anger was there, ready to lash out.

'Oh,' said Stefanie, nonplussed. 'Is he? The Governor? What sort of a scientist?'

'He did cloning,' said Rye, suddenly dull again.

Stefanie opened her mouth, closed it, put down her pen, and got to her feet.

'I'm sorry,' she said formally. 'I apologize. I didn't mean to insult your father.'

He nearly laughed.

'Didn't you? Why not? You do usually.'

'I know. It's got to be a habit. It's because you're so annoying; that, and because the Governor's such a—I mean, because I don't agree with his policies. But Kris said I shouldn't.'

'Did he? Kris?'

'Because the Governor is sort of part of you, so you have to stick up for him.'

Rye thought about it; but the Governor wasn't just part of him. He went all through, like mould through old fruit.

'How long is it since you saw your dad?' asked Rye, suddenly.

She went deep red, knelt down again, and underlined something in her notebook.

'I saw him on the ship,' she said. 'And I saw him at the trial. Not to talk to, but I saw him. And we had nearly two weeks working together before that, before everyone was arrested. Before that, he was on a mission, and before that he was in hiding, and before that he was in prison. I don't really remember much before that. But I've always had newspaper cuttings, and read his books; and sometimes he's found ways to get letters to me.'

'So . . . who looked after you? Your mother?'

'No, my mother died when I was a baby. I went to school. A rather good school, actually.'

'But . . . you've hardly ever seen your dad,' said Rye, unable to imagine it. The freedom of it, to stretch yourself in any direction you liked without obstructions, without feeling guilty, or inadequate, without living in a cage.

Stefanie looked at him, and he saw that she still hated him.

'What my father's doing is really important: more important than us seeing each other. More important than being happy.'

'But . . . he's been put in prison,' said Rye, after a pause. 'So what he's doing—it must be wrong.'

'It's the people who have put him in prison that are wrong!' snapped Stefanie.

And Rye suddenly realized that Stefanie's cage was even smaller than his own.

He took the rest of the crabs off her line, and then he helped her weigh them. And then he went home.

He found that he had to put all his books back into alphabetical order before he could get to sleep.

37

The Governor must have got home some time in the night, because Rye woke to a clanking and *hwoofing* like someone trying to inflate a recalcitrant walrus, and a feeling of entrapment and doom.

It was such a waste of time the Governor heaving sweatily on his exercise machine when he was so greedy. Rye wondered how many jars of marmalade and slabs of butter he'd seen vanish into the Governor's neat little mouth.

It was such a horrible thought it got him out of bed.

A baboon-hooting noise heralded the Governor's shower: and there he was at the table, sniffing violently at his breakfast, seizing his knife and fork, and absorbing food with relish and thoroughness.

Part of Rye.

All of Rye: his future, at any rate; and how could anyone escape his future?

Once the Governor was eating he didn't usually allow anything to disturb his concentration. He shoved large amounts quickly and neatly into his small mouth and chewed fast. And swallowed.

Your family was part of you, Kris had said. Well, it was easy for Kris, who could be proud of the magical caves, of being able to identify an animal by the way it rustled through the grass, of plant lore, of spells, of hunting chants. Rye's father (only not his father: more like his monstrous and bloated identical twin)—what was there to be proud of about him?

159

Governor's orders, Gabriel would say, unquestioning and joyful. But that wasn't enough for Rye any more.

'What are you eating?' demanded the Governor, suddenly, brusquely.

'Yeast extract,' said Rye. He was getting quite a taste for it.

The Governor tut-tutted.

'That's no good. No good at all. What have you been giving him that for, Maria?'

Mum jumped.

'Oh. I didn't know—'

'Well, I've told you often enough! A person needs sugar in the mornings. Sugar, to—'

'Oil the brain,' said Rye, unable to stop himself from sounding slightly sarcastic.

The Governor shot him a look. Then he shifted in his place and rumbled slightly.

'Figuratively speaking, yes,' he said. 'Provides a quick energy boost. You see, Maria? Rye knows.'

'Rye always remembers what you tell him, Ryland.'

Rye looked back down the years. Was that true? Had everything the Governor had ever said sunk into Rye's sugar-sticky brain and taken up residence there? Rye tried to look at his brain objectively, but it was difficult from the inside. There were certainly chunks of Governor-stuff: his body, obviously—how *cruel* was that, how *cruel?*—and other things that came with the body, like being lumberingly slow, so that games had always been a humiliation and a bore; and being always so much the cleverest that you never had to think; and, presumably, having a singing voice like a bull seal with a stubbed flipper. Oh, it was all horrific, cruel, appalling, and totally, totally, totally inescapable.

'Well, have some marmalade now, then,' said the Governor, partially appeased.

160

But Rye didn't want it; his whole being (even though most of it wasn't really his) rose up in revulsion at the thought. But his hand was reaching for the bowl, all the same.

Perhaps I'll throw up all over him, Rye thought, with a flash of hope.

'Come along, come along,' said the Governor, who was waiting, even though he'd disposed of half a loaf of sticky bread already. 'I've got a lot to do.'

Rye's hand stopped.

'I don't think I want any,' he said.

Mum wiped her mouth, quite delicately, but with her finger.

'You're not feeling ill, are you, Rye, love?' she asked anxiously.

Rye thought about it. Sitting at the same table as the Governor was enough to make anyone feel nauseated (only it was sitting at the same table as himself, as himself, as himself) but he didn't think he was ill.

'I don't think I like marmalade any more,' he said.

Rye put his arm back so it rested correctly on the edge of the table. (*Every joint on the table must be cut*: but why, but why? It was just another bit of rubbish that the Governor had put immovably into his brain.)

The air seemed suddenly to have turned to something crystalline, like ice; Rye half expected his breath to form clouds across the glazy tablecloth. Havers stole in and silently extracted the dirty plates. He bent and twisted, as quiet as a shadow, ever so careful not to disturb so much as the air around the Governor.

Rye discovered he had stopped breathing. He folded his napkin and put it quite neatly in front of him.

'Come now,' said the Governor, watchful, but more puzzled than anything else. 'You want to grow up big and strong like your father, don't you?'

Rye took a deep breath, but his voice was somehow out of gear and wouldn't work.

Havers slid expertly round the door while holding a pyramid of plates in each hand. It closed almost silently behind him. Mum started to get to her feet.

'I ought to go and see to—' she began; but the Governor impaled her to her chair with a look.

'I don't,' said Rye. It took a huge effort to get the words out, but once the first ones were said the rest followed more easily. 'I don't want to grow up like you,' he said.

Mum whispered something pleading, but her words reached neither of them.

'Nonsense,' said the Governor, flatly. Then he frowned, rocking backwards and forwards slightly. 'But then I suppose you are getting to the age to be questioning things. Yes, of course you are. Remember doing it myself. Trying time for everybody, ha!'

Rye wanted to hit something—somebody—but the thought of sinking his fist into that soft body made him feel sicker than ever.

'I don't want to be like you,' he said again. 'I don't want to be . . . to be . . . ' but his voice ran out before he could reach the end of that sentence.

The Governor was tapping his fingers on the seam of his trousers. *Light the blue touchpaper and retire immediately.* That was what it said on fireworks. (Long ago, fireworks, on the mainland, when perhaps he'd been freer. Could he go back and find what he'd been then, and work his way older again by a different route?)

Rye suddenly discovered that he didn't want to retire immediately. He felt like a firework himself, flickering and burning and getting ready to explode.

'I want to be different,' he blurted out. 'I want to be—'

Myself: but not myself as I am, but someone else

162

altogether, because someone else is how I would be if I were really me.

Which was nonsense.

(A Governor word.)

'Different?' snapped the Governor, and he was sneering a little. 'Different from what? Different from civilized behaviour? Different from order and—'

Rye didn't know. That was the most frightening, appalling thing. If he'd known what he wanted to be, or even what he wanted to want to be—

'Different from you!' he almost shouted. And that wasn't completely true, either. 'It's not fair,' he went on, angry at everything, everyone, even angry at himself, for sounding like a baby. 'Why did you do it? Why did you do it to *me*?'

He turned to the Governor as he said it and their eyes, their bright blue identical eyes, looked straight into each other and through each other and Rye was somehow lost, drowning, in the infinity of blueness.

Someone said:

'Who told you?'

And someone replied:

'I was reading about Colony Three. It's all there, it's all there, and I'll never forgive you.'

And everything was echoing round Rye so much that it was hard to know whether the sounds were real or in his head; all he knew was that everything was the truth at last; and he twisted and turned and tried to escape because the truth was snapping round him like ivory sharks, round and round, and perhaps he was going to be eaten.

It's only because of me that you are here, Rye.

But I am not here, I am not here. I am nowhere: and I cannot get out.

You could not be anywhere, any other way.

You have trapped me in your body, in your mind.

Given you life, Rye.

But not my own.

Helped you. Taught you.

Taught me to think everything that's in your head!

Rye wrenched his eyes away. His hands, that were the Governor's hands, were shaking.

'I shan't think your thoughts any more,' he said; and suddenly he wanted to cry.

The Governor's face was streaming with sweat, but he was quite calm.

'A most curious phenomenon,' he said. 'Some sort of telepathy, I suppose. If such a thing existed. Which I suppose it must. Interesting.'

Mum looked from one to the other of them.

'I don't understand,' she said.

No, they said together, *you never do*.

The Governor rubbed his hands together cautiously.

'But you're over-stating the case, Rye. We don't think the same thoughts. That was unusual, wasn't it?'

'And we don't spread the same things on our bread,' said Rye, with just a beginning of cautious hope.

'Actually it's not as simple as that. I was never allowed both butter and marmalade at home. We're both rebelling about it.'

Rye thought about this.

'What did your father do?' he asked; and he was amazed that he'd never thought about it before.

'He was a motor mechanic.'

That was the last thing Rye had expected.

'Is he dead, now?'

'Yes, long ago. He died in an accident when I was eight.'

'Oh. What happened?'

'A jack slipped. A lorry came down on him and crushed him.'

Rye had an absurd urge to say *What sort of a lorry*?

The Governor lifted up his knife, ran his fingers along the handle, and put it down again.

'I was taken to see him at the hospital,' he went on, quietly. 'I was very much afraid that he'd be disfigured, but he just looked asleep. Quite peaceful. But they said his brain was dead, and so they switched off all the things that were keeping the rest of him alive. And I remember wondering why they were getting rid of the bits of him that were alive, when I would far rather have kept him, even if he were always asleep.'

'Things happen, when you're young,' said Rye. 'And there's nothing you can do.'

The Governor sighed deeply.

'When you are young, you sometimes want the wrong things.'

'And when you are old you make up your own rules about what's wrong and what's right and so you always want the right ones.'

The Governor let out a sudden bellow of laughter.

'That is supposed to be a secret,' he said.

Rye thought about secrets.

'The colony is failing,' he said.

'I won't allow that to happen. My job is to make it a success. I won't let anything get in the way of that.'

'I don't think you can make it a success, now.'

'What makes you say that, Rye?'

'Come with me and I'll show you.'

38

The Governor's shoes were not suitable for walking on the rubbish-strewn shore. He stood on the sea wall and sniffed violently at the stench of rotting seaweed.

'Aren't there steps?' he asked.

'No, you have to jump.'

The Governor jumped, feet together, ridiculously, almost at attention.

Rye led the way along the beach and the Governor tiptoed after him, prancing and flailing and trying to save the midnight polish on his shoes.

Stefanie was there, with her weighing machine. Rye had hoped she might be.

'Stefanie!'

When she saw the Governor approaching she looked as if she would have liked to jump into the river. But instead she got skinnily to her feet and pushed back her hair where the wind had whipped it free.

'Stefanie's making a survey of the flat-crabs round here,' explained Rye. 'Can the Governor see your results, Stefanie?'

Stefanie picked off the two rocks that were holding the flimsy notebook down, shook off as much as possible of the sand and mud, and handed it to Rye. It was patterned with neat columns of figures.

'You'll have to explain it,' said Rye.

Stefanie swallowed, and pointed a wavery finger at the first column.

'These are the weights of the crabs I've caught,' she began, 'and—'

'I see, I see,' said the Governor. 'And this is the percentage difference in . . . Yes. And here is an average-biased . . . How can you be sure you are not measuring the same specimens over and over again?'

'She's marking them,' said Rye.

'What with?'

Stefanie's pale face flushed deeply.

'A laundry pen,' she said. 'That's all I've got. But it does stay on, I kept a crab in a bucket for two weeks to make sure.'

The Governor looked at her closely.

'So, what does your experiment tend to show?'

Stefanie looked at Rye for help, but he shrugged and kept his mouth shut. So Stefanie had to tell him. The Governor listened with attention; and then he thanked her politely, made for the sea wall, and heaved himself massively and knee-wobblingly back onto the road.

Rye ran to catch him up.

'What did you think?' he asked.

The Governor pursed his lips.

'I think she is a clever young lady. But you shouldn't have introduced her to me: the less I have to do with her the easier it is for both of us.'

Rye blinked.

'But . . . do you think she's right about the plague? That it'll wipe out most of the life in the sea?'

'Quite probably. Quite probably.'

'So—'

'So what? The colony doesn't depend upon the sea, Rye.'

'But . . . all the animals—'

'Will die, yes. But they were certainly going to do that anyway. Everything does. In any case, the development of

167

the colony will be much easier if we don't have to worry about the animal life. People will get so worked up about these things. Ah. Good, there's Willis.'

Rye trotted along beside the Governor. He had felt so close to him this morning, and now he felt as if there was an unbreachable gulf between them.

'Don't you care at all?' Rye asked.

'Care? It doesn't make any difference whether I care or not. Some things have to be sacrificed in order to *have* order . . . And I *will* have order, Rye. Whatever the price. But I'm glad to see you're enquiring into things, setting up a network of consultants, ha! But I shouldn't worry about the crabs on the flats.'

'Harry and Kris have been doing magic,' said Rye, suddenly. 'Magic to protect the island.'

'That's very kind of them, but I believe I can manage the colony quite adequately by myself.'

Rye walked along for a little while, thinking about the island. About earthquakes, and plagues, and the Comm Station. And magic, strong magic, in strong hands.

'The island's too big for you,' he said. 'You know it is.'

'Oh no it's *not*!'

The Governor's sudden rage rushed round Rye, nearly singed his eyebrows off, but Rye hardly noticed it.

'But you don't understand it!' he said earnestly. 'Not properly. Not how it all fits together. Even if no more of the hills collapse, and even if the plague doesn't spread inland, then something else will happen. If . . . if you talked to Harry, perhaps. Harry Shoreman—'

If Rye had sat down for a week and tried to think out the stupidest thing he could possibly have said, he'd have hardly done better than that. The Governor turned on him and the light in his eyes burned away all the air inside Rye and left him gasping and empty. And now the Governor's face was flushed an ugly red; and suddenly he was something else: something foreign, something alien.

Not human any more: bigger than human.

> *Aranui, Aranui,*
> *Netter of souls,*
> *Cast your eyes to the horizon*
> *And let your mighty feet*
> *Pass us by.*

> *Aranui, Aranui,*
> *Destroyer of islands,*
> *Fold your hands:*
> *For we are too small for*
> *Your glory and service.*

The sound of offlander magic sang in Rye's bones long after the Governor had gone about his business.

It frightened him. So he turned his feet up the track to the Shoremans' house, in search of knowledge.

39

Lisa Shoreman was in her warder's uniform. She looked strong and well and there was a peacefulness about her that Rye had almost forgotten existed.

'You're better,' said Rye, filled with wonder.

Lisa laughed, and coughed a bit, and spoke.

'Much better, anyway. I'm going in to work just for a couple of hours to see how I do.'

'Oh, but don't, Lisa. Not until you're properly better. Give it a few more days.'

'I would, but they're in a lot of trouble. The quake caused all sorts of damage—shook the whole place up.'

'It certainly shook *me* up,' said Rye, feelingly.

'It did a good job with both of us, didn't it? But the thing is, they're not too sure how well the construction work has stood up to the shock waves. They've had to herd people together a bit, and that leads to trouble in itself . . . Did you want Kris, Rye? Because he's gone off for a ramble; he's been very good, helping, recently.'

'Then I'll walk down to the prison with you, Lisa. Make sure you're all right.'

Lisa Shoreman smiled, and tucked her hand under his arm.

'Perfect gentleman, aren't you, Mr Makepeace,' she said. 'Just like your—'

Rye asked a hasty question about her shift.

* * *

170

Rye took the direct way back across the hillside, but he found to his annoyance that the red dust rose until it formed a stifling plume around him and behind him, so he progressed like one of the steam engines from long long ago on the mainland. Rye began to go faster: boiling black clouds were appearing over the headland and rain would turn the dust on him to sticky soup.

Rye's nose was soon twitchy and streaming, and that was probably why it took him a while to notice a new edge to the metal-dust smell. He was still wondering if he was imagining it when there was a movement in the fern and a pale streak of salamander ran across his path. It was quite small—perhaps only about two feet long—and it never came within a yard of touching him. But it was unusual for a salamander to break cover that way: generally speaking they lay low until you were about to tread on them.

And now he thought about it the wind was hissing strangely in the grass.

Lots of just slightly odd things, all at once: black, black clouds; a bitter smell; a fleeing salamander; a hissing wind: perhaps they all added up to something, thought Rye, vaguely.

And then there was something else: a growling from across the hillside that mounted steeply to a thin wail, and then to a bellow that pushed at the hills.

Fire! it screamed; and Rye started running.

He pounded through the grass towards the siren, bashing into rocks and tripping over roots as he went. By the time he'd flung himself against the fence of the old prison compound there was a straggly line of blanket-draped invalids slouching palely in lines outside the medicentre, and the six-ton truck was towing the colony fire-fighting trailer through the security gates.

The smoke was going straight up, as dark and fuzzy

171

as Mr Reece's beard, and soon all the people on the colony who weren't fighting the blaze were pushing their noses through the fence. At least it was only the warehouse that had gone up, people were saying, and not the medicentre.

The warehouse consisted of a metal frame covered with canvas, and it went up a treat. Gabriel, who was the strongest person on the whole colony—except, he had to admit, Mrs Hook—arrived very soon, and was kind enough to hoist Rye up onto his shoulders to watch. The flames leapt high into the air, orange and purple and blue. The warders, and the fitter of the invalids, formed a chain of buckets—but you could see the water evaporating into steam before it reached the flames.

It was a good job all the other prison buildings had been taken away, people said, or it would have been a wicked waste.

The Governor arrived quite soon. He immediately ordered all the invalids back to stand in rows where they had been to begin with.

The first explosion happened shortly afterwards. It was so loud that everyone threw themselves on the ground and lay there with their hearts clattering for several seconds. Then they all said *What was that?*

And then everyone remembered that the warehouse was now used as the gas store. Three month's supply of gas, that was. The Governor abandoned the fire-fighting attempt, and people round the fence began to back away.

The next canister to go up took a section of the metal warehouse frame with it: it hung horribly for ages in the air above them and then crashed down almost on the fence.

Gabriel put out a massive hand and pulled Rye to his feet.

'That's it,' he said. 'Time for you to go home, now, Rye. You won't see nothing bigger than that.'

172

Everyone was leaving now. A few of them were making their way up to the ridge for a safer view, but most of them were heading back down to the centre of the settlement.

When Rye looked back for the last time at the leaping, exultant fire, all that was left of the crowd was one small thin shadow with pigtails that jutted out behind it like a frigate-bird's tail. Its hands were clasped onto the wire and it was staring and staring at the ragged lines of invalids.

But what with all the smoke you couldn't tell one from the other.

40

T he Governor only just got home in time for breakfast. His hair was still neat, and he and his belly still formed a magnificently dignified procession. But he was very angry.

'It's all most unfortunate,' he snapped, irritably surveying the breakfast table. 'I've got the men into the ashes to start salvage operations, but it'll be a waste of time. I'll have to start rationing for meat *and* fuel. Great nuisance. And I've had to send everyone home from the medicentre because the heat has melted part of the fence. Still, most of them are more than well enough: they tell me that everybody suddenly got better in the middle of the afternoon a couple of days ago, would you believe. That's the trouble with having a medical officer who's also a criminal, ha! And you know, I wouldn't be at all surprised if he'd had something to do with the fire, except that I can't see what he'd gain from it, apart from causing trouble. Anyway, he's back in the political section of the prison, now, with all his piratical friends. Good thing, too, with that yacht of theirs that's been lurking off the Islets all these weeks.'

'*Is* John Arne really a pirate?' asked Rye; and earned a look that bashed him back against his chair.

'Who told you John Arne was at the medicentre?'

'Um. I just sort of heard,' gulped Rye. Robin Willis had enough problems as it was. The new Comm Station tower had been finished, but Robin had proved to be afflicted with such desperate vertigo that the only way for

174

him to get up or down the ladders was with a bucket over his head.

This was effective, but didn't inspire confidence in the rest of the population of the colony.

The Governor snorted.

'Can't people hold their tongues?' he demanded. 'They'll be telling his daughter next.'

'Oh,' said Rye, with a sickening qualm. 'Er . . . would it matter very much?'

'Telling anyone the whereabouts of the leader of an extremely well-disciplined and well-equipped terrorist organization would seem to be unwise,' snapped the Governor, heavily sarcastic. 'Let alone telling one of his accomplices.'

Mum poured tea.

'I'm sure none of this could be helped,' she said, and earned a look that actually made her duck.

'Obviously not. Or I would have prevented it.'

And Mum tucked away her sympathetic face and fell silent. It had been unusually brave of her to say anything. The Governor didn't like to be distracted by trivialities.

Rye went and found Stefanie. She was walking up the track to the Shoremans' house, and she was carrying books.

'The Governor says your father is a terrorist,' he said, bluntly.

'Eco-warrior,' corrected Stefanie. 'He's fighting to protect the world.'

'Fighting?'

'Campaigning.'

'So your father doesn't actually go about killing people, or being a pirate, or anything like that?'

'Of course not. I mean, I know there have been one or

two odd people in his organization who've gone off the rails and done stupid things; but father's always done everything possible to keep his forces under control. He's always insisted on high levels of discipline.'

Rye thought about the columns of green-armbanded men: how Lotty had said they were nice boys. And how they had changed since the new man had arrived—arrived on the same boat as Stefanie—so that now they only marched, and worked, and kept silence.

'So he doesn't believe in violence, and blowing people up, and all that sort of thing.'

Stefanie tossed her head.

'Of course not. The organization is dedicated to study and conservation. And so, of course, father really hates what the Governor's doing to the island.'

Rye gave her a quick look.

'How do you know? Have you seen your father, then?'

She hardly hesitated for a second.

'When he's in a prison with no visiting?' she asked, so scathingly that her words hit him like a swipe from an angry salamander.

Lisa came out of the house to meet them.

'Kris is out again, I'm afraid,' she said. 'He's gone off somewhere towards the crater with Harry—some offlander magic or other, I think. It's all magic, just lately. I keep being terrified that something will go wrong and we'll end up with the house full of those horrible giant earwigs, or else choruses of petulant gods.'

'I'm sure Harry knows just what he's doing,' said Rye.

'That's more than I am,' said Lisa, with a sigh.

'And, in any case, there's definitely no such thing as magic,' said Stefanie, firmly. 'That's all just nonsense.'

Lisa looked at her, amazed; but then she smiled.

'Well, something's got me better, and that's the great thing. And I'll tell you something else. One of those little

176

dun finches was singing to me the other day, and it told me that it's a special occasion on Thursday.'

Rye looked blank.

'Is it?'

Lisa smiled.

'I don't suppose she's told you, but it's Stefanie's birthday on Thursday. Isn't it, Stefanie?'

Stefanie was suddenly crimson.

'So I thought we'd celebrate. A sort of Stefanie's birthday—me being better—Harry deciding to grow his moustache again—tea party. Four o'clock. Will you come?'

'It sounds brilliant,' said Rye. 'Thanks, Lisa.'

'And how about you, Stefanie? Will you come?'

But suddenly Stefanie's face was as stony as it had been when Rye had first seen her.

'If I'm free,' she said stiffly.

Lisa and Rye looked at each other and shrugged.

Rye followed the sounds of spades until he found Harry and Kris. They were filling in a hole.

'Can I help?' asked Rye.

'No, we finish, now,' said Harry, wiping his brow. 'Good job, eh, Kris?'

'Well,' said Kris, who seemed rather bemused, 'it's done, anyway.'

'Um . . . is it magic?' asked Rye, hoping very much that it wasn't, for the hole must have been at least four feet across.

'Yes,' said Kris.

'No,' said Harry. 'It magic things, yes, lots of power—enough to blow off many heads—but I give it back to island. The gods have more need than I have, I think.'

Rye blinked, and wished he understood.

'And . . . will the gods take the power?' he asked. 'What if Aranui gets it?'

Harry laughed.

'I tell you story of Aranui,' he said. 'One day, man meet god. *Give me power like you*, says man. *Make me fly, then I drop oil-nuts on enemies' heads.* So god goes up cliff with man and says *Jump, you have all power you need.* Then man jump, and he fly.'

'Oh,' said Rye, even more puzzled than before. 'Really?'

'Oh yes,' said Harry Shoreman. 'But only downwards.'

And he laughed again.

41

The penny didn't drop until the next day.

Rye checked it just to make sure.

Arne, Stefanie. Born . . .

Stefanie's birthday wasn't for three months.

What's going on? he thought.

But he didn't think about it hard enough; not even when he spotted Stefanie up on the hillside doing something to her cairn. He just prayed to every god of the island that her love-spell house was nothing at all to do with him.

The Governor was not to be seen about in the settlement for several days: now that the river was diverted back to a safe route he had switched his attention to the Comm Station, and he was standing over Robin Willis and had no attention for anything else.

'Here,' said Mum, very quietly, to Rye, glancing back over her shoulder. 'Take this envelope to the store, and Mr Reece will give you a package to bring back here. Do you understand?'

'It doesn't sound all that complicated,' said Rye, who never minded a chat to Mr Reece.

'No,' said Mum. 'Rye!'

He looked back, his hand on the door handle.

She came close and spoke quite softly.

'Don't let Dad see you, whatever you do,' she said.

Mr Reece took the envelope and flicked up the flap with a grimy thumb.

There was a lot of money inside it: Rye was genuinely startled. Mr Reece smiled a thin, satisfied smile, tucked the flap back in, and settled the envelope in the inside pocket of his overalls. Then he ducked down behind the counter and came up with a paper parcel.

It was surprisingly heavy, and its weight flopped and shifted in a quite unexpected way. Mr Reece put his finger against his nose, winked, and patted his pocket happily.

Rye carried the parcel away. He really didn't want to know what was inside it, but the smell teased him irresistibly, until at last he made for the dry end of the old river channel, slithered down under the cover of the ferny overhang, and carefully unfolded the ends.

The salamander had had its feet and head cut off to make it easier to parcel up. The skin had gone dry and black.

There were also four pentagon crabs, large and heavy and illegal and not quite dead. Rye's heart thumped when he saw them, even though he'd known they would be there.

He looked down across the long grass. There must be half a dozen men with lines on the beach.

Everyone knew that the Governor was fully occupied at the Comm Station.

I will have order, the Governor had said.

But he'd been kidding himself. He might have sorted out the erosion of the hills by the river, but there were so many other problems. There was Harry, with whatever big magic he'd done; and the Comm Station still down; and the plague that might spread anywhere; and the people of the colony, who would take whatever they could get away with, and never bother about the future.

If there was a future.

A shadow fell on Rye, and he jumped; but it was only Gabriel.

180

'Look,' said Rye, squinting up at him against the light. 'All those men out there are fishing for pentagon crabs.'

'Yes,' agreed Gabriel, rather heavily, 'I guess they are.'

'So . . . are you going to tell the Governor?'

Gabriel sighed, and sat down on the edge of the channel, so that Rye found himself looking at his huge muddy boots.

'That's not my job,' he said.

'But—'

'I just do what I'm asked, Rye, as well as I can, and leave all the thinking to others. That way I don't have any worries.'

Rye felt suddenly very tired.

'Sometimes that's not enough, Gabriel,' he said; and he wrapped the parcel up carefully again and carried it home.

'Good boy,' said Mum, scuttling down on him and taking it carefully. 'This'll cheer Teresa up. And, Rye, Dad didn't—'

'No,' said Rye. 'He didn't.'

Mum blew out a sigh of relief and hurried back to the kitchen.

42

The Governor nodded appreciatively.

'Good,' he said. 'Very good. What is it?'

Rye hoped very much that he hadn't just eaten that blackened and shrivelled salamander.

Mum managed a smile.

'Crab fricassee, Ryland,' she said. She had spent the whole meal perched on her chair as if in momentary expectation of it exploding.

'Excellent, excellent. Has Rye been fishing? Don't tell me that Charlie Box has ceased his battle on the slugs for long enough actually to do something useful.'

'Oh, no. They came from some people in the settlement. I had to pay.'

'Well, good for them: their rations are going to need a bit of variety now we've lost so much food in the fire. It's good to see people ready to act for themselves.'

'Everyone knows they have to look after themselves a bit more because you're so busy at the moment,' said Rye.

'Quite right. Quite right. At least—I suppose I can't be everywhere.'

'What was that?' asked Mum, still horribly nervous.

'What was—?'

'There it is again,' said Mum. 'Up on the hillside. Not another earthquake, surely.'

The Governor had stopped chewing.

'Doesn't sound like it,' he said.

There was a distant pattering, like gravel on a window, but drier-sounding.

'It sounds like fireworks,' said Rye. Perhaps a ship had been sighted. It had come because the mainland hadn't heard from the colony for so long; and so they were letting off fireworks to celebrate.

The Governor got suddenly to his feet, even though nothing, nothing, nothing was allowed to interrupt his meals. He went to the window, found it only looked down to the sea, and walked swiftly out of the room. His napkin, that he always left folded on the table, fell like a little ghost behind him onto the royal blue carpet.

There was another pattering from far away. And then another. Then silence.

Rye suddenly discovered he was afraid. He hoped that any moment now the Governor would come billowing in and make some snorting comment about some idiocy or other of someone's.

But there was the noise again. Up on the hillside, as Mum had said.

'Sounds as if it's up by the prison,' said Mum, who had relaxed a great deal since the Governor had left the room.

Rye went to take a sip of milkless tea and then realized he didn't want it. He muttered something to Mum and went after the Governor.

The Governor was peering out of a window through a pair of binoculars.

'What's happening?' asked Rye, though he had never wanted to know something less in his whole life.

The Governor glanced round, put down his binoculars, and then took them up again.

'Don't know, yet,' he said.

Then he said:

'Go quickly and get your mother and the servants and take them all down to the Comm Station.'

Rye stood for a second while his heart lurched clumsily and fell somewhere cold. Then he turned and went.

'What?' said Mum. 'The Comm Station? What, me as well? Oh, all right, then. I'll just pop and powder my nose, and then—'

'No,' said Rye. 'You've got to come now.' And he took her by the hand and led her along to the kitchen.

Havers the butler was just pouring something tawny into a very small glass, and Teresa was scrubbing furiously at a soapy plate. Mum went over and picked up a tea towel.

'I'd better help you with those,' she said. 'The Governor wants to take us down to the Comm Station, and—'

Charlie Box came in suddenly through the door to the garden. Amazingly, he wasn't carrying anything that looked as if it might be a slug-trap, and he seemed almost agitated.

'Here,' he said, 'there isn't half a rumpus going on up by the prison. Smoke, and people running about.'

A wave of coldness washed through Rye.

'We were wondering what it was, ourselves,' said Mum, comfortably. 'The Governor's looking into it. It's a good thing we'd finished dinner, isn't it?'

'They're coming down this way,' went on Charlie. 'I don't like the look of it, to tell you the truth, and that's why I came in.'

Mum held up a glass to the window to make sure it was properly clean. She found herself looking through the distortions to the garden gate.

There was a man at it. He was wearing an orange boiler-suit and a green armband.

She gave a little scream and dropped the glass. It smashed on the metal treads of the floor and Rye thought, *Too late*.

They were too late.

He struggled to accept the finality of it. Pirates, a band of them, disciplined, trained, outside. And that sound that he had thought was fireworks—had he really been as innocent as that, only five minutes ago?

'There!' said Mum. 'What a clumsy old thing I am! But that man, he gave me such a start. Whatever are they doing moving prisoners about today? You'd think they'd have enough to do, what with the Comm Station and all the other troubles.'

Rye, just for a second, sent up thanks to all the gods that Mum was really no relation of his; then he went along the wall to the window and pulled the blinds closed.

'Lock the door,' he said, 'and keep away from that window.'

Then he left them.

The Governor had closed his blinds, too. The light shone through them to where he sat in an armchair. It cast blue shadows on his face and made his rosy cheeks look dark; and Rye was suddenly so scared that even breathing hurt.

The Governor looked across and smiled; and for the first time ever there was no bustle, no energy, no restlessness.

Rye wanted to go up to him and shake him.

'We can't get out,' Rye said. 'There's one of the prisoners at the gate, and there are more coming down the hill.'

He kept hoping that the Governor would say, *We'll have to take the secret passage, then*; or *Yes, we'll have to throw smoke-bombs to cover our retreat*; or some other brilliant scheme to sort everything out.

But the Governor said, quite placidly:

'They're all round the house. About thirty, as far as I can see. Armed, too, some of them. They must have got access to the prison armoury. It's all been very well planned. I thought I had everything under control, Rye; but you were right. It was too big and I missed something. I'm sorry.'

Rye stood and breathed fast and told himself he was ready for anything.

'What shall we do?' he asked.

The Governor smiled again, and ran a slow hand down Rye's arm.

'I think we'd better give them what they want, Rye. And then I think they'll go away.'

Rye's heart went bump-bump-bump-bump.

And then he realized.

'No!' he said, in horror. 'No, you can't—'

But the Governor was heaving himself to his feet.

'I don't know what's happening elsewhere,' he said. 'But everyone must get out of here as soon as there's a chance. Don't go to the Comm Station, that may well be their next target. Go to the Hostel, first, and then, if you can, make contact with Harry Shoreman: he'll be able to take you all somewhere safe. One of those caves of his that I never managed to find, perhaps.'

Everybody was ready in the hall.

'My dear friends,' said the Governor. And he shook hands with Havers, and Teresa, and Charlie Box, and Miss Last.

'I've got a good sharp spade,' said Charlie, doughtily. 'I'll soon show 'em!'

'Thank you, Charlie, but there's no need, just now. Maria—'

Mum was struggling to get her arm into her coat. She could never learn to do it nicely, but always flapped about like a chicken in a sack.

'I'm coming with you,' she said.

The Governor laughed, quietly, as if that was truly, delightfully amusing.

'Maria,' he began, 'Maria, you don't—'

'Oh yes I do,' she said. 'I know I'm slow—and stupid with it—but we've had hard times before and I've always been with you.'

'I'm afraid you can't come this time,' said the Governor.

She suddenly started to cry.

'But I can't manage without you!'

'Then you must do the best you can,' said the Governor; and put his hand on the handle of the door.

Rye looked up at him.

'You'll be killed,' he said. It was a brief statement of fact.

And the Governor nodded, quietly, as if it didn't matter, much.

'But you won't,' he said; and opened the door.

43

Rye stood with his forehead against the cold wall and wished he had the courage to look out of the window. But every second told him it was nearly too late, and nearer too late— In the end the noise and wailing of the others drove him out of the hall and across the royal blue carpet past the Governor's armchair to the closed blinds.

He slid them open onto a lonely world. No one. And he felt empty and hollow, just like the hills: as if the tiniest tap would cause him to collapse in splintered ruin.

He leant close to the glass, and then he saw something. A whole group of men in lurid boiler-suits. A few of them were walking backwards, and those ones were carrying rifles.

There was another man among them, but he was surrounded and Rye only got a quick glimpse of dark hair above a dark suit.

Stupid clothes for hill-walking.

And there—there was someone else: another stranger amongst the prisoners. There was a smaller figure that ran and jumped and seemed full of joy and energy.

Stefanie.

Rye's knees were trembling, suddenly. So he sat down on the armchair; curled up on it. There was just a little warmth left in it, perhaps. He stayed there until the warmth had leached away or else mingled with his own.

Havers gave him a drink. It was so foul that it shocked him properly into the world again.

'Dad said we were to leave,' he said dully. 'Put on some warm clothes, everybody.'

'I'll do us a supper to take with us,' said Teresa, resolutely.

Of course. The Governor would have thought of that.

'And we'd better take us a blanket each,' said Havers.

That too.

'Yes. Blankets, and any food we can carry,' said Rye. 'Nothing else. We're leaving in five minutes.'

Rye went into the Governor's office and turned on the computer. He changed the password.

On the filing cabinet there was a photograph of the three of them, all very smart, taken years ago at the Governor's Investiture. Rye picked it up, hesitated, and then left it. There was nowhere safer.

Everybody was waiting in the hall. Havers had unearthed from somewhere a pair of plus-fours and some fiercely hairy stockings.

'We're going down to the Hostel,' said Rye.

Havers nodded magisterially.

'Yes,' he said. 'We must band together. Protect the womenfolk.'

Rye wavered. He didn't want to band together. He wanted to get away to a dark place where he could curl and mourn and not have to do anything.

But what he wanted didn't matter.

He stepped out of the door and sniffed at the evening. Rain, soon, probably: but not quite yet.

'Leave the door open,' he said to Havers, who was fumbling with a bunch of keys.

'But—'

'They'll get in anyway, if they want to,' said Rye bleakly. 'And if they start smashing things they won't stop.'

'It's all happening again,' said Mum, shivering. 'It's

189

all falling apart. I prayed it wouldn't, but it is. Oh, why did he bring us to this dreadful place when we were so happy?'

Rye took his mother's hand and led the way down the road.

44

The settlement looked empty, but the wide hills felt full of eyes.

The Hostel was quiet, but when they were nearly at the gate there was a dry *tap!* from up on the prison track and something singed the air beside them.

And then the top of the gatepost stopped being there.

Instantly, violently, amazingly: huge splinters of wood rocketed up, and the gate lurched suddenly forwards on one hinge.

Rye had dragged Mum past the twisted gate and was round the corner of the building before he had time to think about anything.

Then he thought, *Is everyone all right?* But his feet didn't even consider stopping to find out. He saw an open doorway, lunged at it, and found himself gasping and panting in a mildewy kitchen. The doorway darkened behind him as the others crowded in, and then people were pushing their way past him to stack tables and chairs against the door. Rye stumbled forward out of their way and found himself in a dark corridor where planks had been nailed across the window. He went through an open doorway into a wide room full of tables and the smell of drink. There were little pictures everywhere of large women.

'Rye!' called Gabriel's voice. 'Rye, thank all the gods! Where's the Governor?'

But someone had already told someone, and the news was sweeping through the room. Gabriel took a deep breath when he heard it; but then he drew himself up straight.

'All right,' he said. 'All right. Then we all have to do the best we can. Think. Think for ourselves.'

Rye sat down in a corner and listened as hard as he could. Anything to stop himself thinking. So he listened to the men, and he listened to his own heart beating; because he had an obscure feeling that if he could keep his own heart beating, then Dad's heart would keep beating, too.

'All we *can* do is shoot,' Mr Reece was saying, pulling at his beard. 'You can't talk your way round a bullet.'

'The difficulty is, we don't know what's happened up at the caves,' said Havers, shaking his head. 'We've got a group of about thirty prisoners on the loose—but where are the rest? They might still be locked up. Or there might be fighting going on up in the caves now.'

'And some of those men out there are violent criminals!' piped up young Kevin Frost from across the room. 'Eco-pirates. They won't stop at anything, they've proved that. Bombs, throat-slittings: and they're waiting out there to come and get us. We've got to knock 'em sideways. Wipe 'em out before they wipe *us* out.'

'But they've taken the Governor,' said Robin Willis, uneasily; and there was silence.

The wide room suddenly blurred and dimmed. Rye got up and blundered his way half-blindly through the maze of chairs and out of the room into the corridor.

He saw some stairs and went up them. The first flight was carpeted, but the next was bare boards. At the top was a hatch-like door. He pulled it open and climbed through.

It was Stefanie's room. It must be, it was too small for anyone else: the fern-sack bed was barely five feet long. Everything was completely neat. There was a nastily pink stuffed bear, pristine and totally unloved, on the bed: but there was no clutter on the cardboard box table. Not even a hair brush.

Rye opened the front flaps on the box.

Nothing.

He sat back, blinking.

She wasn't coming back.

That was why the prisoners had gone back over the hill. They'd left a couple of men behind to keep people cooped up in the Hostel, but the rest of them were making their way—where?

There was a small window over the bed. Rye looked out. There was no sign of anyone on any of the hills: but that didn't mean there was no one there.

Even as he thought it, there was a *crack!* from somewhere and the great dustbins by the Hostel wall jostled and clashed.

That was just a warning. A warning from someone invisible out in the empty island.

But just a minute, there *was* someone out there. There was someone huddled down by the fence, though the wooden uprights broke up his outline and made him hard to make out.

Kris. It was Kris, out in the open where people were firing rifles.

Kris, not shut up with the women and the farmers.

Rye cursed, and blundered down the stairs again to the dark passage. He headed towards the kitchen, but then he remembered that the door was barricaded, and that Mum and Annie and the others were there. So he wrenched at one of the planks nailed across the window until it came loose and sent a shaft of light to illuminate his neat pink hands. Then he attacked the next plank, tugging and twisting until it came away so suddenly that he stumbled back against the wall. More light spilled in and made the crimson carpet glow.

He reached through and got the window open, and then he squeezed through the gap between the remaining planks, hoisting one heavy leg out through the opening and forcing down his head. He swung himself outwards, lost his balance somehow, and slipped sideways and mostly hands first onto the sodden ground.

He lay there, breathless, and horribly out in the open: the only thing that stopped him climbing back inside the Hostel was that he was too frightened to get up. So he heaved himself over to Kris on his stomach, as cumbersome as a seal. His T-shirt came untucked as he went, and the thin mud scraped itself slimily along his stomach.

Kris pulled him into the shelter of the fence.

'What do you think you're *doing*?' he asked, almost angrily.

Rye hadn't the faintest idea.

'Well, whatever it is, you shouldn't be doing it here,' said Kris. 'Come with me!'

Rye pushed himself into a crouching run and went after Kris. Rye swerved heavily through the gate, nearly fell over on the mud, and pounded on clumsily down the path past the store.

There was a drainage ditch by the main warehouse. Gabriel and Clarissa had scoured it out so long ago that it was overhung with weeds. Rye, purblind with fear, put a foot wrong and went down into it like a sack.

Stefanie was there. Her eyes were glistening.

'I was wrong,' she said. 'I came back. I'm not on anyone's side.'

45

Rye kept trying to breathe, but his windpipe seemed to have filled up with gravel, and it was difficult.

'He wasn't who I thought he was. My father. He was someone else,' said Stefanie. 'He'd said . . . he'd said we'd escape; just get away. That's what I helped him do. He didn't say people were going . . . it's not right for people to get hurt. That's what it's always been about, to stop things getting hurt. That's what I thought.'

Rye took the deepest breath he could and managed to say, *Is Dad . . . ?* before it ran out.

'They've taken the Governor hostage,' said Kris, steadily. 'He's probably the safest person on the island at the moment.'

'Then . . . where are they taking him?'

Stefanie was a hunched shape in the dimness.

'Up to just beyond the mouth of the estuary,' she said, dully. 'There's going to be a boat to take us all off. It's been doing a survey round the Western Islets, and I signalled to it. My father gave me a short-range transmitter: I got to see him after I cut my arm, you see— it wasn't Annie's fault, she didn't realize who he was— and Lisa and some of the other warders carried messages for us. Not that they knew what they were doing, of course, because it was all in code—my father told Lisa it was going to be my birthday, but that was really the date for the escape, and there were other things like that. But I helped with it all, and it's all going to work perfectly. It's all really clever. But my father and the others were talking

. . . and . . . once we're on the boat . . . the Governor won't be safe then. So I came away.'

Rye began to get out of the ditch, but Kris stopped him.

'Wait a minute,' he said.

'But I can't—'

'—do anything useful,' said Kris. 'We need help, lots of help. Listen. Dad's shadowing John Arne and the rest of the eco-pirates. He sent me back with Stefanie so I could let people know what's going on, and I expect there'll be an expedition to rescue the Governor. The prison's back under control, now, but they haven't got many staff to spare because there's been a lot more damage. Anyway, the boat isn't due to pick up the prisoners until sun-fall tomorrow, so there's plenty of time. You can go along with the rescue mission, Rye.'

'No I can't,' said Rye. 'They'd never let me.'

'Nor me,' said Stefanie. 'And I must go.'

Kris was silent for a moment while he digested the truth of this.

'Then we'll go together, by ourselves,' he said. 'Look, you two set off along the beach now. Don't walk on the dry bit, it's too noisy: you'll have to paddle through the mud. And turn your T-shirt inside out, Rye: those white bits will show up for miles. I'll meet you by the seal rock. All right? Wait for me there.'

Rye and Stefanie waded along the empty shore. There was an occasional *crack!* of a rifle.

'It's all right,' said Rye, steadily, 'it's all right. It's too dark for them to see us.' But the mud glistened faintly in the mean light of the cloudy moon, and it was hard to know what eyes on the dark hills might see.

Then there was another cracking shot, much nearer, this time: it split the clouds into drenching rain and for a moment it stopped Rye's heart.

It stopped his heart.

Rye felt blindly for Stefanie's hand, and pulled her on.

They had waded half a mile when a lean shadow detached itself from a chunk of rock that had fallen long ago from the hillside and said:

'Hello! Rye? Stefanie?'

'How did you get here so quickly?' asked Stefanie, almost angry. 'How did you get past us?'

'Offlander stuff,' said Kris.

46

'Here,' said Kris.

Rye blundered against the dark rock wall, found the opening, and banged his head going through it. It was pitch black inside. He put his hands out in front of him and slid his feet along until he reached the wall on the other side.

'Is this where we came before?' he asked.

'Yes.'

There was a scrape, and a match flared, steadied, and moved through the blackness until something shone back at it. Dirt-grained fingers opened the front of a hurricane lamp and put the match to the wick.

Rye blinked round as the light flared up. The cave was full of gear: sacks of food, and sleeping bags, and even cups and plates.

'Why have we come here?' he asked.

'To rest.'

'But—'

'Just a few hours, Rye. We'll need it. And we can eat here, too.'

'But we'll still get there in time?'

'Yes.'

'But in time for what?' asked Stefanie. 'In time to get caught in the crossfire? This is so incredibly stupid I can hardly believe it's happening.'

She looked from one to the other of them and threw her hands in the air. 'Everything's inside-out and stupid and *wrong*,' she said. 'My father's planning to kill Rye's father,

198

and Harry is probably planning to call down a curse on both of them. And here we are, together; and I've no idea why *we've* stopped fighting each other. Perhaps we still should be.'

Kris heaved a sigh.

'No,' he said.

'But why not?'

'Because Kris would win,' said Rye. He got to his feet. 'I'm going further in.'

The yellow lichen-light was even more amazing when outside it was dark, and lashing down with rain. Rye stood in the middle of the animal cavern and gazed at the salamanders and snakes and lizards that twined around the walls.

And there, over there, was something different. It was big, and he thought it was a whale for a moment; but when he looked again it was a man: a fat man, with dark hair, weaving his way effortlessly between a coiled snake and a salamander's elegant tail.

'I thought he should be there,' said Kris's voice, suddenly, behind him. 'I thought—all this is supposed to be magic. It's supposed to make things work together. So I thought—'

'I think he's dead,' Rye blurted out, and the words wrenched all his insides as he said them. And then he told Kris everything. Completely everything, even about what had happened on Colony Three.

Kris listened until the end. Then he led the way into the next chamber.

'See,' said Kris. 'The pool is still here: the earthquake didn't touch it. Or the quenchers. And look!'

He lowered his cupped hands into the water and brought up a little pool that squirmed and then stilled with a life of its own. Rye peered in.

'There are thousands of them,' said Kris. 'A whole new generation.'

They were just a blob of translucent jelly with a lashing tail behind.

'They're incredible,' said Rye.

Kris lowered his cupped hands back into the pool and let them swim away.

'But not magic,' he said. 'I'm not sure that any of this can be magic.'

And he led the way back to the darkness of the first cave.

47

Kris woke them two hours before moonfall. They ate stale bread washed down with spring water: every rock was gushing gallons after yesterday's rain. Then they each took a rolled-up blanket and a bag of stuff that Kris had sorted out for them and set off.

There were dark smudges of cloud flying low over the hills: one moment would be clear, and the next a flight of wet fog would swipe contemptuously across their faces. Kris led them across the hills and at one point they lay on their stomachs and looked back down at the scatter of houses and buildings of the settlement. Amongst the hills and the great expanse of mud that stretched nearly to the horizon the buildings looked hardly more than toys.

'I expect Gabriel and the others are well ahead of us,' said Kris, 'but we can take short cuts and catch them up.'

Rye closed his eyes and there was the Governor mincing along the road in front of him, his tie over his shoulder, shouting greetings to everyone. He would be busy, busy, busy, in his stupid shiny shoes and sunset-tie.

Rye opened his eyes and the road was empty.

'Let's get on,' he said, curtly.

Kris led them, slipping and sliding, down a scree slope to gather a fleshy-leaved plant that grew in the shingle, bouncing against the boisterous wind.

'Are you sure you can eat this stuff, Kris?' asked Stefanie, wrinkling her nose at the smell.

'Oh yes. It's legendary, bladderleaf is.'

'What sort of legend?' asked Rye.

'Mostly the sort that involves the words, *things got so desperate that they were reduced to eating bladderleaf*,' admitted Kris. 'It'll be the most revolting thing you've ever tasted.'

This was quite a claim, and in fact it wasn't that bad, being a bit like string flavoured with burnt rubber, with just a hint of cabbage-eater's wee.

'It's not that much worse than whale pie,' said Rye, champing gamely; and then suddenly, for no reason at all, he found he wanted to cry and cry and cry. He rubbed his forehead hard to give himself something else to think about.

But then Kris said *Shh!* and froze into stillness.

48

Kris was staring back and across the hills.

'Quick,' he said. 'Quick.'

Kris and Stefanie turned down the hill, and Rye struggled along behind, tripping over the ends of his blanket, and with his over-loaded bag swinging about and bashing his knees.

He was nearly at the bottom of the valley and balancing his way across a stream-bed before he got a chance to look back.

Two men.

Two orange men.

Quick.

Kris and Stefanie were out of sight, now. Rye stumbled after them, huffing and wheezing like . . . like nothing. Run, run, think about that.

And here was the shore, with the cliffs coming down either side of it.

And they were trapped.

What could they do? What *could* they do?

But now Kris and Stefanie were diving into a clump of big ferns and hauling at something. The raft, of course it was. They were dragging it with clumsy haste across the shingle and down to the shallow lapping water.

But that was mad. To set off on a home-made raft . . .

There was a *crack!* behind him that echoed twice off the hills and Rye stopped worrying about anything else. He rushed the last few yards and threw all his weight against the raft. It slid onto the mud, bounced on the shallow water, and skidded away.

'Quick,' gasped Kris. 'Load up!'

They threw their blankets and bags onto the raft and followed it into the sea with the mud slipping and squirming under their feet. Then Rye put his foot into a hole, fell forward, and went right under water.

He came up splashing and coughing. After that they swam, holding on to the raft and kicking their legs.

The raft began to move faster once it caught the main channel which snaked through the expanses of shallow water and mud.

'Any later and we might have been stranded,' said Kris. 'We'd better get up on the raft before it gets away from us.'

They were as careful about it as possible. Kris and Rye steadied one side of the raft while Stefanie wriggled her way onto the opposite one; but even with every care the thing tipped very nearly disastrously as Rye heaved himself aboard.

At least now the raft was so heavily loaded it was much more stable than before. They sat, chests heaving, and let themselves drip. The raft rocked along the channel, turning idly, sometimes catching on the edges of the mud, but always twisting itself free again until the channel widened and joined others, and they were being pulled along on the outward tide between the low cliffs of the estuary that bent sharply away from them.

'This is mad,' said Kris, suddenly. 'We should never have done this.'

'What?'

'Come out so far. We're nearly halfway to the sea.'

Stefanie looked back at the colony; it was only a smudge of grey at the end of the mud.

'We'd better put in again,' she said.

'How? We can't steer this thing. And it's too far to swim.'

Rye looked to see how far they were from the shore.

Too far. Much too far.

He tried to heave his mind on to the problem; but his brain was feeling as cumbersome as his body did.

'When the tide turns it'll take us back up,' he said.

'If we're not out at sea,' said Kris.

Stefanie looked round wildly, as if she were expecting a path to appear, or a boat to come into sight.

'We can't go to sea on this thing!' she exclaimed. 'We wouldn't last ten minutes!'

Rye said nothing, but bowed his head so it hung down close to his beating heart.

49

B ut the sea was perhaps even more mysterious than the land. The great waters took the little raft and spun it like a leaf. It swirled it onto an ocean stream as flat and glassy as a mirror and then lost interest in it and left it becalmed in the wide jaws of the river.

Rye was the first to stop vomiting. He lifted his head unsteadily. The light was strong, now. His mouth tasted foul, so he rinsed it out with sea water. He even resisted the strong, strong temptation to swallow.

He and Kris had tried drinking sea water years ago; they'd made themselves very sick, but then it hadn't mattered, except that Mum had worried and fussed and Dad had laughed at them.

He'd laughed.

Amongst their gear was a groundsheet and a small bucket. By the time Kris and Stefanie were interested in anything, Rye had rigged up a water-collecting device: rain would run down the groundsheet into a plastic-bag funnel and end up in the bucket. It wasn't elegant, but it would work.

It worked quite soon: cold rain came down in a vigorous and compact squall. Rye had worked out their water-collection drill, and they were able to collect more than half a bucket of water before the squall rushed inland and left them to cope with the newly choppy sea. They drank the water straight away. It wasn't enough.

The day went on forever. The next rain woke them too late to do much about it; perhaps it had never been much, because the sea was only rocking gently, like a giant cradle.

'How far out are we?' asked Kris, shading his eyes.

'A couple of miles?' guessed Stefanie.

'Do you think you could swim it, Rye?'

'No.'

Stefanie sighed.

'It's crazy: here I am, actually wanting to get back, when all I've been longing for ever since I got here is to leave,' she said. 'Look at it. Isn't it grey and bare and awful?'

'Long ago,' said Kris, suddenly, 'when my father's people first came here, the whole island was covered in forest. There was a sort of tree that bore a nut that could be sliced and eaten like bread; and there were lots of different fruit trees; and there was a bush whose branches could be split to make fabric and rope; and there were fat ground-birds so tame you could catch them with your hands.'

'So what happened?' asked Stefanie.

Kris shrugged.

'My father's people were greedy. They chopped down the trees and didn't bother to plant more: and then, when they found there wasn't enough to eat, they chopped down more trees to make spears to fight each other for what food there was. And in the end there was only one tree left on the whole island; and so they chopped it down, and built a boat, and sailed away on it. And I'm sorry they made such a mess of things.'

There was a pause while they imagined it.

'None of that was anything to do with you,' said Stefanie.

Kris nodded.

'I know. Because I was born a century too late. By the time I got here there was hardly anything left to destroy.'

Rye spoke loudly, to keep his voice steady.

'Well, Dad's been finishing the job off,' he said.

'But not out of greed, or vengeance,' said Kris. 'Only because there are things he doesn't understand.'

'Of course,' said Stefanie. 'And things he doesn't know he doesn't understand. That's when it's really dangerous. I thought . . . father . . . well, I was wrong, anyway. I thought he wanted to save the world; but all he really wanted was to have everything done his way. And I helped. Did all sorts of things.'

'That wasn't your fault,' said Kris.

'Yes it was. If I'd thought about it I'd have worked it out. It's almost funny: all I did was what I was told. That's what they say all the time, isn't it? *Do as you're told.*'

'Perhaps that's what we're born for,' said Kris, soberly.

Stefanie snorted.

'They should all get dogs,' she said, scathingly. '*Sit, stay, fetch.*'

'*Grow up to be what I wish I'd been,*' said Kris.

'*Believe this or be forever banished.*'

'*Endure the agony because I did.*'

Rye sat up and looked at them with a feeling as if he'd just awoken.

'Is it like that for you, too?' he asked.

'Of course,' said Stefanie. 'It makes no difference whether you're a clone or not.'

That startled him completely.

'How did you—?'

She shrugged.

'It was fairly obvious. Cloning was your father's speciality, and he was in the Colony Three disaster. Didn't take much brain to work that out. Anyway, I only had to look at you.'

'But that doesn't matter,' said Kris, earnestly. 'You know it doesn't. I mean, if a—if a *twin* kills someone, you wouldn't put the other one in prison as well, would you?'

Rye shook his head, not in disagreement, but to try to shake away his confusion.

'He wanted me to be him,' he said, slowly. 'That was why I was born: so I could be him and carry on what he was doing.'

Stefanie suddenly lost patience completely.

'Well, he failed,' she said. 'Every parent does. My father decided I'd be most useful to him as a scientist and a warrior for nature. And I have been. I've been measuring things since I could hold a pen to write down the results, and spying for him, and doing all sorts of things: whatever he said. And where has it got me? Here. Drifting about with you two, about to die of thirst or else of being capsized and torn to pieces by an ivory shark. And do you know what? I reckon I've wasted an awful lot of the life I've had.'

Kris nodded.

'And my father brought me here so that I could be a real offlander,' he said. 'To learn the magic, even though half of it's nonsense, and most of the other half's for killing things. But I'm still supposed to be a proper illiterate offlander, when the offlanders' main achievement has been destroying most of the life on their island—and that includes nearly all the people.' He paused, then went on slowly. 'But we don't belong to them. They can't own us. We don't have to believe what they believe.'

'But . . . Dad's gone . . . and I feel . . . ripped in two,' said Rye, and his voice was raw.

Stefanie and Kris looked at each other again.

'That's not because you're the same person as your father,' said Kris, a little wearily. 'That's because you love him.'

'Twit,' said Stefanie, softly, to underline his words.

50

A new current caught them, and made the little raft bob and tip and swirl. Kris succumbed to groaning seasickness almost immediately, but Stefanie hung on, as white as a gull's wing.

'We're closer in,' she said, through gritted teeth. 'Tell me we're closer in.'

Rye peered at the cliffs.

'There have been massive rock-falls along here,' he said. 'Quite recently, too: must have been the earthquake.'

'I don't care,' growled Stefanie. 'Just tell me we're in closer to the shore!'

Rye looked again.

'Actually, I think we are,' he said.

'But still too far to swim?'

'Much too far.'

The sea did strange things: it would be choppy one moment, threatening to slide them all into the sea; and the next it would be shimmering under the grey sky while they raced towards the shore; and then, frustratingly, it would whisk them away again across the metallic gleam of the water.

'Could we use the bucket as a paddle?' asked Stefanie. 'It might help a bit.'

But it only sent them round in circles until Rye, in disgust, ripped half a plank off the raft and used that on the other side.

'No,' said Kris, raising an unsteady and horribly green face for a moment. 'Paddle next-door to each other. Make one of the corners the bow.'

It took a fair bit of readjustment, but it was worth the trouble. They could still hardly move the raft at all, but when they got caught in a contrary current they were able to steer their way through it to some extent.

'Can we swim yet?' asked Kris, the colour of dead bladderleaf.

'Not yet.'

'Can I drown, then?'

'Not at the moment, Kris. We'll let you know.'

Another shower hit them about noon. They gave all the water they collected to Kris, who was still being sick. He was so ill he didn't even realize what they had done. Rye felt heroic about this for several minutes; but it wasn't long before he went back to feeling weary to death, and thirsty, thirsty, thirsty. He and Stefanie paddled for five minutes and then rested for ten. If by any chance of tide and wind and current they happened to be going towards the shore they paddled constantly to try to get some speed up.

'Inertia,' panted Stefanie. 'It'll carry us on.'

Rye doubted it; the flimsy raft was hardly more than a piece of driftwood, and it was almost entirely at the mercy of the wind and water. He kept firmly in his mind a picture of all the driftwood he'd ever seen washed up on the shore.

'Look!' croaked Kris, at last. But he was still flat on his stomach, and his eyes were closed.

'What at?' asked Rye, seizing the excuse to stop the futile paddling.

'People,' said Kris, without moving. 'A whole clan of people . . . with a great machine that makes its own road.'

Rye and Stefanie looked at each other.

211

'He's really ill,' said Stefanie, uncertainly.

But Rye shook his head.

'I think it's magic,' he said. 'Kris! Can you see anything else?'

There was a long pause. Stefanie went to say something, but Rye waved her quiet.

'Travellers. They come out of the hell-pit that devours the sun.'

Rye turned and looked west. And there it was, a big yacht, riding the waves strongly, plunging along to its rendezvous. Then he turned and scanned the hills. He couldn't see Clarissa, but there was a lone figure standing silhouetted against the sky. It was holding out his arms to them.

'Kris,' said Rye, 'there's Harry up on the cliff. I think he's—'

But now there were men coming down out of a fold in the cliffs and onto the beach. They must have rubbed their clothes with mud, but the orange of their uniforms still showed through.

Rye stared and stared while his heart thumped and juddered and his lungs failed to take in any air.

Yes. There he was. Very far away, and very, very small. He was so small that Rye put out his hand, as if to pick him up.

'Listen!' said Stefanie, sitting very upright. 'That's Clarissa, isn't it?'

A chugging, a purring, came to them over the water; and it was such a familiar sound.

'But they won't be in time,' said Stefanie, suddenly.

Rye glanced back. The yacht was charging down on the group of little men on shore; in comparison Clarissa was a snail. A frigate-bird in a race with a snail.

They would knock Dad on the head and tip him overboard.

212

'There she is!' said Stefanie.

Kris had been right, Clarissa had a whole clan with her. It was too far to be quite sure, but surely that was Mrs Hook with a club swinging from her hand.

The sails of the yacht shivered, and then the yacht swerved aside from its path and came to rest about thirty yards from the shore. Sometimes the waves took the raft high enough for Rye to see the men on board.

Kris suddenly sat up. His eyes were wide with shock.

'They're coming!' he said. 'The cousins of the sea. My father has called them. Quick, quick!'

He seized the bit of wood that Rye was using as a paddle and began to drive it into the water. The raft kicked under them and actually began to move.

'What?' said Stefanie.

'*Taraloina*,' gasped Kris. 'Quickly!'

Rye grabbed the bucket from Stefanie's hands and started sweeping it back through the water with all his strength.

'What?' said Stefanie, again, but Rye didn't have any energy to spare to answer her.

Taraloina was one of the very few offlander words he knew.

Taraloina: the cousins of the sea; the grey hunters; the hate-eyes; the dagger-mouths.

The ivory sharks.

A great form slid past them, hardly greyer than the water. It was bigger than anything should ever have been.

'It left us,' whispered Stefanie. 'It left us!'

Kris didn't stop paddling.

'Soon the sea will be boiling with them,' he said; and Stefanie made a noise as if someone had knocked all the breath out of her.

'My father!' she gasped. 'He won't know. Kris, they'll all be wading out to the yacht and *they won't know*!'

Rye dug into the water with all the strength he had.

The heavy glinting sea rose, swelled, and fell again, and the ivory sharks slipped massively round the little raft. Again and again a shark would sweep aside the water in its path and make the raft tip heart-stoppingly sideways, and Rye and the others would throw themselves down, clinging on for dear life.

The shore was perhaps a hundred and fifty yards away, now: but it might as well have been miles. Kris was as white as a bone.

'Can't go on much longer,' he muttered. 'The raft's too heavy, anyway. We're not moving it, Rye.'

'Oh yes we are,' said Rye, fiercely. 'We're going to get there.'

'Let me have a turn with the paddle,' said Stefanie.

'Sit down!' snapped Rye, turning on her, furious with urgent fear.

Stefanie went white, then, but Kris took a gulping, steadying breath.

'Rye's right,' he said, palely. 'Sit down, Steff. It's all right. I can carry on for a while yet.'

'But—'

'It's important you keep your arm away from the water. If the sharks scent blood—'

Another shark swept vastly by them, its dorsal fin breaking the surface for a moment. It was scarred, and rough as sandpaper, and heavy enough to smash the raft to matchwood without feeling it. Rye snatched his hands clear of the water.

'Kris!' said Stefanie, in a voice that was suddenly as

thin as a ghost's. 'Can *you* do something? Some sort of . . . of chant?'

But Kris only bowed his head.

'I'm sorry,' he whispered. 'But there's nothing. I've been thinking, but there's nothing at all. Steff! There's not any . . . *science* . . . is there?'

And then it was Stefanie's turn to bow her head.

Rye looked at the cliffs. They were perhaps a little closer, but only a little. His arms were aching badly, now, and every time he put his hands near the water he expected a mighty pair of jaws to rear out of the water and tear them away. But he wouldn't give up while there was a chance. Not while the sea was full of hating eyes; not while the prisoners were marching towards the flesh-ripping sea, and Dad was with them.

'Pray to the gods,' he said. 'We can't do anything for ourselves. Pray to the gods to help us.'

And they pulled their way in minuscule, painful inches towards the cliffs to the yearning accompaniment of Kris's offlander prayer.

The end came with absolute suddenness. One moment Rye was waiting wearily for a wave to swell under them, and the next the whole raft had flipped, and they were flying.

Rye hit the water, went down deep, kicked, and bounced up again. He shook the hair out of his eyes and looked round. A couple of plastic bags bobbed up emptily around him. There were bits of wood around him, too: planks that had once been the raft.

He grabbed a couple. The waves were lifting around him and he couldn't see far. He shouted.

'Steff! Kris!'

And there might have been a reply, but his ears were full of water. He swam a few strokes and grabbed another plank of wood.

215

A great cold shape came close, closer, and then, with an ungainly swerve of its body, vanished again into the greyness of the water. Rye, shoved aside and under in its wake, tumbled, righted himself—and there was Kris, gasping and wide-eyed and kicking, and looking all round. They saw each other, but then Kris deliberately turned away from him and swam, calling *Steff!* and turning round and round in the water. Rye turned, too, looking, and trying not to think about the cut on Stefanie's arm. If it still had even the slightest trace of blood about it . . .

And then she was there, in front of him. She had a bruise on her bumpy forehead, and she was moving slowly and feebly. He plunged towards her, snatched at the easiest part of her, which was her hair, and managed, after a huge teeth-gritted struggle, to wedge one of the planks under her shoulders to support her. He was trying to do the same with another when he heard a shout.

'Rye! Look! Look!'

Rye turned his eyes to the shore. But the cliffs were still a hundred yards away, and the sea was interwoven with huge sliding hate-filled shapes, and Stefanie was hurt, and it was too far.

But Kris was bobbing up next to him and grabbing his arm.

'Look, Rye! Look there!'

A wave came and lifted him; and he looked. And he saw that the island had extended a wide path of glistening mud almost to their feet, as if to take them in.

51

They made it to the first hummock of tough grass and then they collapsed, gasping and gasping. Rye allowed himself just enough time to get a little of his breath back; and then he pushed himself up, failed to make it to his feet, and tried again, harder. His legs were so heavy and clumsy that they hardly seemed to belong properly to him.

He slogged through the muddy dunes until the top of the mast of the yacht came into view again. Another fifty yards of stumbling, and there on the beach was the group of prisoners, and the dark bulky figure of Dad amongst them.

And there was Clarissa, with her cabin wrapped round in corrugated iron like a crazily eccentric tank, and half the people of the colony: Gabriel, and Robin Willis, and Mrs Hook, and Annie, and Mr Reece, and Charlie Box, and loads of the others.

They were standing, the two groups of them, facing each other across the muddy shingle. And then there was a sharp order from somewhere and the prisoners began to walk backwards towards the sea. Three of them had rifles, and one of them was pointing towards Dad's head.

Rye had thought he had no energy left to run any more, but he was running now. And Stefanie and Kris were running too, so that they arrived tumultuously together on the beach.

'Don't!' screamed Stefanie. 'Father! Stay where you are! The sea's full of sharks!'

'My father called them,' shouted Kris.

And now Gabriel was appearing from inside Clarissa's cabin and stepping forward, hands raised in token of peace.

'All right,' he said. 'Let's all stop for a moment now. The important thing is that no one else is—'

Someone fired a shot that whizzed through the air like a high-powered wasp and bent one of the roof-poles of Clarissa's cabin. Gabriel took three quick steps forward, but someone shouted *No!*

And after a moment Rye realized that it had been two voices that had spoken: he looked across the shingle to a man too far away to see properly—a man dark at the top, then pale, then dark again, who bore a bright strip of silk like a sunrise. And he knew that their voices had spoken together.

But Stefanie was running past Rye and on towards the prisoners.

'Father,' she called, 'it's true! Harry Shoreman called them.'

Rye would have followed her, but a voice close in his head said *No!* again. So he stopped, breathing fast and somehow not sure quite where he was.

Stefanie was right among the prisoners, now.

'I've seen them,' she said, very urgently. 'Ivory sharks. Harry called them. He did the shark-chant, and they've come. You mustn't—'

And then a tall man with a bony forehead was grasping her by the shoulders and shaking her just a little. And Rye saw it all, heard it all, close, close, even though he was too far away to see or hear it at all. And it was very odd, because he was looking down on Stefanie, as if he was much taller than she was. And she seemed suddenly very precious, and very young.

The tall man was speaking. Rye was far away across

218

the beach, but he was seeing everything from somewhere else, too: through another pair of bright blue eyes. He could see John Arne's shoulders rising with each breath, and he could feel inside himself the thudding of a heart much heavier than his own.

'That's nonsense. Nonsense,' John Arne was saying. 'You know it is. A man can't call a shark. All the sharks are miles away, in their spawning grounds.'

Stefanie looked up at him, her dark eyes burning in her pale face.

'I've seen them,' she said. 'They're there. I know they shouldn't be, but they are. I'm sorry, but it didn't work. I'm sorry. You'll have to come back.'

But the man's hands tightened on her shoulders so that she flinched and even tried to pull away from him.

'It isn't *possible*! Don't you understand? There's no such thing as shark-chanting. There's no magic. We don't need magic, when we have nature. That's what we are following, Stefanie: not man's way, but nature's way.'

'But you don't know what it is!' said Stefanie, suddenly really frightened. 'You can't do. Let me go!'

'Let her go!' said Rye, although it was not out of his own mouth that the words came.

But John Arne caught up his daughter and swung her round towards the sea and the waiting yacht. She screamed: and Ryland Makepeace, with a vision of the lithe grey bodies that wove the sea across with a barrier as sure as steel, lunged out after Arne, and caught him; and then somehow they had fallen, and rolled, together, and then apart, and somehow Stefanie was in his arms.

But then something hit him very hard, and the whole world came rolling and spinning together in hot, hot colours.

Another earthquake, Ryland sort of thought, as his senses faded: and this time it has caught me.

It seemed almost fair, although the pain of it was exploding round him like a silken sunrise.

And all around him people were shouting, were screaming; but when at last he managed to open his eyes all he could see was the lapping of the red, red sea.

It must all be because of him, somehow—because everything was because of him. His fault.

So he welcomed the night.

'Rye! *Rye!*'

Rye blinked at the shingle and tried to work out where he was.

'Are you all right?'

He wasn't sure: it was very strange, because he knew he was perfectly all right; and yet he was somehow sure he was unconscious and injured at the same time.

Rye shook his head and came back properly into his own self. Kris helped him up.

'I'm fine,' Rye muttered. 'I'm fine.'

He looked around.

The prisoners were lying face down on the shingle and Mrs Hook was standing menacingly over them, her club in her hand.

'There was a scrap,' explained Kris. 'The prisoners were going to swim for the yacht, until . . . until they saw what happened to John Arne.'

Rye remembered the colour of the sea that had lapped before his father's eyes. He looked round for Stefanie. Annie was with her. And there was Mum, kneeling by a dark figure that lay huddled on the beach.

'The Governor got knocked on the head,' said Kris, quietly. 'We don't know quite how badly hurt he is, yet, Rye.'

Rye took a deep breath.

220

'He'll be coming round soon,' he said, his eyes back on Stefanie. 'The broken collarbone's the worst thing.'

Kris gave him a sharp look.

'How do you know that?'

Rye shrugged, and began to make his way over to the others.

'Magic,' he said.

52

Rye woke much later from an exhausted sleep, and sat up in panic when he saw the moon-glinting black water so close to where he lay; but then he felt the roughness of the ground under him and he remembered.

The shingle was hard, and so he heaved himself up. A little way along the shore he found the bucket cast up and he realized that he was parched. So he followed the sound of trickling water until he found a place where the black rock was soft with moss and letting fall a little cascade of splashing water. He cupped his hands under it and drank and drank and washed his head and knew that he would value every drop that passed his lips for the rest of his life.

Clarissa had borne the Governor back to the settlement. Gabriel had tried to persuade Stefanie to go with the others, but she wouldn't.

'I promise I won't run away,' she told Annie and Gabriel; 'but I want to be with Kris and Rye while I can. And I need to sleep. Please.'

The morning found the three of them alone on the shore without a shoe between them, or anything to eat. So they chewed industriously on bladderleaf.

'At least this only *tastes* of wee,' said Rye. 'There were times yesterday when I thought I was going to have to—'

'Don't,' said Stefanie, shuddering.

They started to walk. They headed back along the muddy shore, picking their way through the huge islands of fallen rock that were still as sharp-edged as razor shells.

There was plenty of water. It trickled down through the rock in spurts and waterfalls through carpet-trails of ferns and moss and tiny starry flowers. They all kept stopping to drink and drink, just for the luxury of it.

At one place, where a great spout of water leapt out of a jumble of fallen rock, Rye said:

'What are all these shoots, Kris? They look much juicier than that blasted bladderleaf. Can you eat them?'

Kris glanced at them; and then he looked again, more closely.

'No idea,' he admitted. 'I've never seen anything like them before. They're odd, aren't they? They look as if they want to grow upright: and nothing does, round here.'

Stefanie put her head close to the strong shoots that had grown so fast that they were still pink from the darkness, and whispered: *Go back, go back, the wind will bend you and the rain will lash your roots away.*

Rye cleared his throat and made an attempt at injecting some sanity back into the conversation.

'All this is newly exposed,' he said, gruffly. 'See, a whole chunk of the cliff has come away. The seeds might have been buried in the watercourse for years and years, and now they've only just got to a place where they can sprout.'

'Yes,' said Kris. 'It's possible, if they need light to germinate.'

And then a thought hit Rye so hard that he gasped. He dug his fingers hard into the crumbling rock and carefully scooped out one of the delicate pink shoots, rubbing the fragments of rock away until the thready root-structure was exposed. They were growing out of a black spherical thing the size of an ice-gull's egg.

He suddenly felt tears prickling his eyes.

'They're trees,' he said.

53

They climbed the last hill as the light was turning soft with the approaching evening. It was steep, and they were very tired.

Stefanie stopped at the top and looked down over the settlement.

'I've spent all my time here hating everybody,' she said.

'No,' said Kris. 'You helped Mum, didn't you, and showed me reading.'

'Hating Rye, then,' said Stefanie. 'Rye and the Governor.'

Rye took a deep breath.

'Things like that happen sometimes,' he said. 'It's just because you're looking at them from the wrong place. It can't be helped.'

They went down the hill. Kris stopped just for a moment when they came to the track that led off towards his home.

'I don't know what to say,' he said. 'Except that everyone is really truly sorry about your father, Stefanie. And that I'll do anything I can to help.'

Rye and Stefanie went on. Their feet were sore.

'Will you tell the Governor that I am grateful,' said Stefanie, at the Governor's gate.

There were things Rye wanted to say. But they were all tangled up, somehow, and he couldn't find an end to start him off.

'What happened . . . it was all a jumble. I'm sure that . . . your father . . . if Dad could have—'

Stefanie swallowed suddenly, hard.

'I'm very grateful,' she said; and turned and made her lonely way down to the Hostel.

They gave Rye food, and a bath, and endless lectures about how foolish he'd been. Even Charlie Box felt entitled to have his say.

'You shouldn't have gone off from the Hostel,' he said. 'Letting that Arne girl lead you into trouble. It's a good thing for you that the Governor's poorly, or you'd really be for it.'

When Rye woke next morning the house was very quiet. Far away there was the clinking of elaborate china being placed on the table for breakfast, but there was no *hwoofing* or puffing or clunking.

Mum hesitated when Rye asked how Dad was.

'I don't know,' she said. 'Not himself.'

'But I thought he wasn't that badly hurt.'

'Well, he's not, really, Rye, love. He's got a nasty bump on the head, and, of course, his collarbone's broken. And that's really painful, or so I've been told. Enough to lay anyone low, I suppose.'

'Except Dad,' said Rye.

Mum managed a small smile.

'He doesn't want any breakfast,' she said. 'He hasn't had anything to eat since they brought him home. It's not like him, Rye. He's bound to be tired, I know; and I suppose he is only human . . . '

'Brand new thought for the day,' said Rye; and bit into some toast.

There were people visiting constantly. Mostly they were just making kind enquiries, but there were also people who needed help, or advice.

226

'I'm very sorry,' said the Governor's wife, again and again, 'but he's resting. If you'll leave a message . . . '

Rye looked in on Dad in the afternoon, but he seemed to be asleep. His face was turned towards the wall, in any case, and he didn't open his eyes even when Rye said his name.

The next day Rye woke again to silence, and so he did on the next. Rye's feet were recovered enough by then to ease on his oldest, softest shoes; and he was about to go out in search of Gabriel and Clarissa to see how badly her cabin was dented when Robin Willis came in.

'How's the Governor, Rye?'

'I'm not sure, really,' Rye admitted. 'Is it something urgent?'

'More like a catalogue of things than something . . . I know he got slugged pretty hard, but I thought that other than that he wasn't much hurt. Look, Rye, could you talk to him? Tell him I need to see him. I'll make it brief, but we're ready to start testing the Comm Station, and I need to know what to report when we get through.'

Rye took a deep breath.

'I suppose I ought to see how he is, anyway,' he said.

Robin Willis patted his arm.

'Good boy,' he said. 'I'll wait.'

The curtains of Dad's room were closed and the place smelt closed-up. And rooms with Dad in them were never like that: he always imported a brisk breeze wherever he went.

'Dad!' said Rye; and got the same answer as he'd got whenever he'd tried before, which was none at all. Rye thought about going out to Robin Willis and reporting failure; but instead he went to the window, drew the curtains firmly, and opened the window wide. The warm island air blew through the room and Rye felt better at once. He went to the bed and surveyed the pink and be-shadowed figure lying there.

'Are you in agony?' he asked, abruptly.

Dad opened his eyes, and then winced away from the light. That rattled Rye quite a bit, because Dad wasn't one for wincing away from anything.

'Robin Willis needs to talk to you,' Rye went on. 'Let me help you sit up.'

But there was a sling tied round Dad's neck, and Rye wasn't sure how to do it in case he pulled something out of true.

'Look,' he said, at last, a little impatiently. 'You can't just lie there. People need you. Robin does, especially. He reckons the Comm Station will be going live soon.'

The figure on the bed spoke, quite calmly and flatly.

'Tell Robin I've resigned.'

It took a couple of seconds for Rye to believe it. He stood for a moment and imagined telling Robin Willis just that. Then he said: '*Tell him yourself!*'

But Dad's bright blue eyes only blinked at the white ceiling.

'Very well. Bring Robin here, then.'

Rye looked at him. His plump cheeks had fallen into dull blotches and he was untidy and unshaven.

Rye felt suddenly ashamed of him.

'I'll wait till you've washed,' he said, firmly.

Gabriel was waiting with Robin Willis when Rye went to hunt out Dad something to eat. By the time Dad was bathed and changed and sitting in his dressing gown with his breakfast in front of him, Mrs Hook had joined them. And by the time Rye had cajoled Dad into eating, Harry Shoreman was there, too.

No one disputed the lady's right to speak first.

'It's about Steff,' said Mrs Hook, hoisting her terrifying bosoms so she could fold her arms. 'She's not much

228

trouble, really, and we don't mind having her, even though she really is a moody little madam a lot of the time and she's always moaning about us not having a proper library. But the thing is, it was all right when it was just while her father was banged up; but now he's passed away we feel more responsible. She needs proper schooling, and a proper home.'

'No arguing with that,' said Gabriel. But Dad didn't say anything at all. He sat and gazed at his paunch, quite peaceful, and quite calm.

'I'll note it down for consideration as soon as possible,' said Robin Willis, hastily, very alarmed. 'Rye, would you be kind enough to show Mrs Hook out?'

By the time Rye got back Robin Willis was tearing his hair out.

'But you can't resign *now*,' he was saying. 'I need decisions on . . . a dozen things.'

Dad was still calm. And he was never calm.

'Well, make them,' he said, patiently.

'But I can't! No. No, I just can't. Even if I were in a position to be able to, I couldn't.'

Dad sighed. It might just have been his sling, but he looked bent, and suddenly quite old.

'Then choose someone among you who can. Gabriel, here, perhaps. He's very well liked, and he's done more practical good on the island than anyone, and he's certainly proved his qualities of leadership.'

But Gabriel had taken a step backwards and was putting his hands behind him.

'Oh no. Oh no, not me, sir. I'm glad if I was a help when it came to the fight, but I can't give Mr Willis orders, nor anyone else. No one in their right mind would take orders from me. And anyway . . . and anyway, me and Annie . . . Annie says we ought to be getting married. And we can't, without there being a Governor to marry us,

229

can we? Anyway, the Governor, he needs to have big brains. Not like me: though it's true that sometimes I was so placed that I could see things that you couldn't, sir, and now I wish I'd upped and told you what was on my mind. But that's why the Governor needs big brains: he needs to understand what's going on.'

Dad managed a melancholy smile.

'That certainly disqualifies me,' he said. 'Look, my governorship has been a disaster. I'm the man that introduced the pentagon virus into the sea, for a start.'

'Yes,' said Gabriel. 'And that was pretty stupid, I'll agree with you there, sir. But the pentagon crabs have all gone, now.'

'And we think the plague virus must depend on the pentagon crabs to keep on re-infecting the other animals, because the sea's looking healthier already,' said Robin Willis, helpfully.

Dad was frowning.

'Gone?' he asked.

Gabriel nodded vigorously.

'Yes, sir, every last one. Why, the men have been out every day while you've been so busy at the Comm Station and they've taken every single crab. Very good eating, too—or so I've been told.'

'What?'

Dad sat up, and his eyes even shot out a small flash of lightning; but his collarbone must have twinged, for he sank back again, wincing and nodding.

'A good thing,' he said, judiciously. 'A good thing. Isn't it, Shoreman? What you wanted. Why, you did your best to kill all the pentagon crabs as soon as they arrived.'

Harry Shoreman hesitated, and then shrugged.

'I wanted the island to stay the same: like offlander times,' he said.

'There you are. There you are, then. There's someone who understands the island. Make Harry Governor,' said Dad. 'He knows more about the island than anyone.'

Harry Shoreman gaped; then he laughed. And laughed.

'Live like offlanders?' he said. 'You crazy? Split each other's skulls, like men in grave? Cut down trees and make wilderness? OK, I call sharks, they come; but you taste shark? It worse than Mr Reece's whale pie, I tell you. Yes, some things I know. There are trees growing where the earth has fallen. They should be moved, planted, yes, I know where, how. And there are other plants which would grow here well—plants for food, for selling, for pigs to eat—you wasting your time with grass crops, Mr Makepeace. I show you all that. And I show you magic, one day, perhaps. Not much, most is for killing; but some magic there is, to make island strong, happy.'

'That's right,' said Robin Willis. 'We need Harry. Of course we do. But he won't do as Governor.'

'He certainly won't. He cooks too well,' said Gabriel, as if putting the matter beyond question.

'Governor must be big ideas man,' went on Harry. 'Lisa, she say you have new scheme, yes? Prisoners who escape tell her. Make space for them: for exercise, growing things. Give them land when they are freed. That good scheme. Lisa say so.'

'Yes,' said Gabriel, nodding. 'It takes a big brain to come up with something like that.'

Dad half smiled.

'My big brain caused the earthquake that killed fourteen people,' he said.

'And now you're making the best of a bad job,' said Robin Willis. 'That's what this place is all about. Let's face it, practically everyone on the whole colony is here because they can't manage to live on the mainland. We're nearly all ex-convicts, and the place was nine-tenths

231

destroyed when we got here . . . it's a miracle that any of us can manage to keep ourselves alive.'

But Dad only shook his head.

Then Robin Willis and Harry and Gabriel all looked at one another, and none of them had anything else to say.

But Rye did. He walked over to Dad and stood half in front of him, facing the others, as if protecting him.

'Stop pestering him,' he said. 'It's not fair. I know him better than any of you, and he's not up to the job. He never was: just be grateful he's finally realized it.'

Rye glanced back at Dad for a moment.

'I know, because we're so much alike,' he went on. 'Exactly alike. And I know Dad's stupid, really, because he's just like me.'

Dad shifted uneasily in his seat.

'He's a coward, too,' said Rye, inexorably. 'And a bully. Just like me, you see; I've inherited it all. He only ever came to the island so he can manipulate people. So he can watch them suffer.'

And now the fingers of Dad's good arm were drumming against the seam of his dressing gown.

'But now he's fed up with being in charge,' went on Rye, 'so that's that. It was only ever about doing what he wanted, you see. We're both like that. Not caring about anyone else, not even our own—'

'All right, all right!'

It was relatively minor for one of Dad's explosions, but still it was like someone switching on an arc-light.

Everybody stepped back and squinted at him.

'Very well, very well,' said Dad, irritably at the boil. 'You've made your point, Rye. But I'm right, all the same, do you hear me? I'm just a fool. And if you're all determined to be governed by me then I don't think much of your intelligence, either, any of you.'

Robin Willis shrugged.

232

'So what else is new?' he asked.

'All fools together,' said Harry Shoreman, nodding and grinning. 'That's how it must be, always. A community, yes?'

Gabriel, beaming, stepped over and shook Dad by the hand. It wasn't easy because Dad only had his left hand available for shaking.

'That's right, that's right,' he said, smiling and smiling. 'You're a big man, Mr Makepeace. We may all be fools—but you're the biggest fool of any of us!'

And at that the Governor began to bounce up and down, like the lid on an over-heated saucepan, as, very carefully so as not to jolt his bones, he began to laugh.

54

Stefanie had no near relatives.

'No thank you,' she said to the Governor. 'I know none of what happened to father was your fault, or Mr Shoreman's, either, but I don't want to live with either of you. It wouldn't seem right.'

The Governor nodded.

'Very well. I'm sure you're aware that Annie and Gabriel are willing—keen—to have you with them,' he said. 'And I expect you'll be a help to them with the new arrival.' And he made a mental note to find some excuse to adjust Gabriel's wages accordingly. 'But you'll still be doing lessons here with Kris and Rye, in any case,' he went on. 'And that's every schoolday, without fail, do you understand me? Think of it as a sort of corrective custody.'

Stefanie was a blasted nuisance to have lessons with. She was infernally clever. Rye found he even had to do some reading in the evenings, sometimes, just so he could be properly relaxed during the day. Luckily Stefanie took every possible opportunity to boss Kris into catching up with the Schedules, so that gave Rye some breathing space.

The Governor was very busy. There were a thousand things to do, and so he did them, even though his collarbone took a long time to heal and his cheeks were grey with pain by evening. Rye did what he could to help. He reported on the careful excavation of the rock-falls, and the establishment of the new forest. He took notes and

234

messages and he fetched things. He was nearly as busy as Mum, who was organizing the wedding and kept bothering Harry for flowers to make confetti, or getting people to cut horseshoe shapes out of old packing cases. And she had begun knitting little white things that Rye didn't even want to think about.

'Come fishing,' said Kris, for the tenth time.

Rye heaved a sigh.

'I can't,' he said, regretfully. 'Dad'll want stuff taken down to the Comm Station. They haven't got the stairs put together yet and he can't manage the ladder one-handed.'

'So, let Robin go,' said Kris. 'Or Miss Last, or Charlie. Come on. I found the oil-barrels from the raft washed up the other day and I thought we could have a go at building another one.'

Rye's eyes widened.

'Your dad'll kill you!' he said.

Kris looked thoughtful.

'I don't think he's quite as traditionally offlander as all that any more,' he said. 'But anyway, *you're* all right, aren't you? Your dad's got his arm in a sling. If I were you I'd make the most of it.'

And Rye was very much tempted; he didn't go, though, but carried on doggedly running errands, not even stopping to chat to Annie, nor to help with the repairs to Clarissa, nor to admire Murray and the newly-recovered Lotty's new vegetable patch—but instead driving everyone almost mad with the resigned and virtuous long-suffering on his face.

55

'How far can the Governor walk?' asked Kris, one day, when Rye's foul temper had caused Stefanie to stamp off home and even Kris's own mild nature was causing him some discomfort.

'I don't know,' said Rye. 'He seems quite a bit better. I suppose he could walk most places.'

Kris nodded.

'All right, then. I'll take you both somewhere. Will you ask the Governor? Tell him it's important.'

'Where?'

'It's a secret. An offlander place.'

He wouldn't say any more.

Their way lay into the centre of the island. There was nothing here but endless hills of endless grass and fern.

'It'll be forest again one day, though, won't it, sir?' said Kris, adjusting his long stride to something more suitable for plump and delicate middle-age. 'We've transplanted nearly all those trees, and said prayers over them, and we've found four more kinds already. Dad thinks that one of them might be the oil-nut tree.'

'Then we must hope that the gods will shower their magic upon the project,' said the Governor, politely.

'Not all of the gods,' said Rye, hastily. 'It'll be best if some of them keep away.'

Kris gave him a sharp look.

'Really? Which particular ones, Rye?'

236

Rye realized he'd put his foot in it. He blushed, and tripped over a fern root, and mumbled *Aranui*.

Kris's face cleared at once.

'Oh,' he said. 'Yes, I remember. *Aranui*.'

'Is he . . . she . . . it . . . a particularly powerful god?' asked the Governor.

Kris made an apologetic face at Rye.

'Aranui's not a god, sir,' he said. '*Aranui*—well, *Aranui* just means *proud man*.'

Rye stared at Kris, indignation swelling inside him.

'What? You mean . . . and all this time you've been letting me . . . *why you*—'

'How much further is it?' asked the Governor, hastily, putting an affectionate but restraining hand on Rye's shoulder.

'Over the old lava-flow, sir, and we're there.'

It was just a wide shallow pool like any of a thousand others on the island.

'If you'll just wait for a minute,' said Kris. 'Here, sir, sit here, on this clump of grass. This pool is famous as a place of healing, and I'm sure it will make you feel better. That's it. I won't be long.'

He came back clutching a smallish salamander in each hand. They were black, with a handsome yellow stripe down their backs, and bright green eyes. He gave the one which wriggled and kicked to Rye, and the other to the Governor, who raised an eyebrow and put the salamander on his lap, where it sat quite happily.

'This sort of salamander only lives just here,' said Kris, 'just round this pond. I think all that rough lava we had to cross to get here forms a barrier to them—it dries their skin out. That makes sense, doesn't it?'

'I suppose so,' said Rye, guardedly.

'OK. And these are both females, OK?'

Rye looked.

'Yes,' he agreed.

'Right. You know my knife, don't you? My best one, with the crab-picker on? Well, I'll give it to you to keep if you can find me a male.'

Rye stared at him in wonder.

'Sounds like a good offer, to me,' said the Governor.

So Rye got up and began to search.

There were hundreds of salamanders. Hundreds: and they were mostly dead easy to catch. Rye looked for a long, hot half an hour, and then he twigged it.

'The males spend all their time in the pond, don't they?' he said.

'Have a look,' said Kris, who was lying, irritatingly relaxed, by the Governor's feet.

There were a million tadpole things, and huge amounts of toe-tickling mud; but not a single salamander.

Rye waded out, dripping, and rather cross. Kris was sitting peacefully beside the Governor, who was looking better than he had for ages.

Rye scowled at them.

'I suppose they're all in burrows,' he said.

'No,' said Kris. 'It's all solid rock two inches down.'

'So—are you telling me the males are much bigger and can get over the rock, after all? Because I think that's cheating.'

'No.'

Rye cast about in his mind for some other alternative.

'They can fly,' he said. He knew it was impossible and he wasn't surprised when Dad laughed, though he was very glad; he even found himself smiling ruefully. He took off his T-shirt and wrung it out.

'All right,' he said. 'I give up. Where are the blasted males?'

Kris looked at them.

'There aren't any,' he said.

'What?'

'The females give birth without needing males. Oh, it's definitely true, they've been kept by offlanders for generations. But it means that they're all the same. Just the same. I suppose you'd call them clones.'

'Oh,' said Rye.

'But look at this,' said Kris.

He pointed at the salamander that was still sitting on the Governor's lap.

'See? That toe on the front right foot? It's been broken, hasn't it, and it's not mended properly. And look at this one.' He dived at a salamander that was regarding them from a clump of grass, but it leapt forward with a flick of its tail and he missed it completely. 'OK, that's a fast one; but *this* one's really tame, isn't it? And look at this one— gotcha!—it's got an extra stripe down its flank.'

Rye pulled his damp shirt back over his head.

'I see,' said the Governor, suddenly. 'Rye, do you understand? Do you see? Do you understand what it means?'

Rye blinked, and thought about it.

And then he knew.

'It means I'm going to design excavators when I grow up,' he said. And he looked at his father, a little sorry.

Ryland Makepeace put his salamander on the ground, and it scuttled away.

'That really would make me proud,' he said.

Also by Sally Prue

The Devil's Toenail
ISBN 0 19 275310 X

I thought that if I held the devil's toenail in my hand, and I looked at it, perhaps, really close so I got cross-eyed—and if I concentrated really hard, then maybe I'd pick up this dark power and . . . and it'd be just so cool.

Stevie is determined to be part of the gang, to be in control. But to be accepted he has to do things—difficult things, scary things. And then he finds the devil's toenail. It's only a fossil, but it seems to give him power—power to impress the gang, to overcome his fears, and to be what people want him to be—or maybe it'll just help him to be himself, whoever that is . . .

'I'd like to suggest you read this without pausing for breath.'
    The Bookseller

' . . . a dark, intriguing and powerful book.'
    Publishing News

'Scary and thrilling, and quite impossible to put down.'
    Irish Post

'Another great book by Sally Prue. A thought-provoking, shocking and very well-written story, and a really good read.'
    Reading Is Fundamental

Cold Tom

ISBN 0 19 275272 3
ISBN 0 19 271887 8
Winner of the Branford Boase Award

Tom had never been to the city of the demons before, and it smelt of death. He stood and shivered by the bridge over the river, his skin prickling with danger. It was madness to cross— but then he was in danger if he stayed, too. He slipped across on the shadowy side.

When Tom has to run away from the Tribe and the common where he has lived all his life, he escapes to the city of the demons, full of its chariots and houses and noise. The demons are so different from the Tribe, with their clumsy ways and their coarse, loud voices—Tom doesn't want anything to do with them. And he certainly doesn't need their help, because he is wild and free, and won't rely on anyone for anything.

But he does need somewhere to hide. And he soon finds that just because he's not interested in the demons, doesn't mean the demons aren't interested in him . . .

'Inventive, originally and distinctively alarming. A very fine first novel.'
> Michael Morpurgo

'This is one of those rare, strange, wonderful books that makes you see the world through different eyes.'
> *The Guardian*

'*Cold Tom* by Sally Prue offers a different look at the worlds of humans and elves . . . an enthralling and original book.'
> *The Bookseller*

1

The Tribe fled. Tom, frantic, heaved himself into the purple branches of a scrubby blackthorn and held himself as still as he could.

There were three of them. Demons. Not especially large, these ones, but heavy, hot, gross—blaring at each other with ugly voices.

Tom did his best to quieten his breath. How had demons got here? He hadn't been asleep, he was sure of it. He should have seen them long ago.

They were heading this way. They made enough noise with their trampling—so why hadn't he heard them before?

They were coming back into sight round a tangle of hawthorn, and now he could smell them, musty and foul. They kept touching each other, holding each other, casting slave-shadows into each other's minds.

Tom held his breath so he wouldn't be sick.

They were going to pass right underneath him. Tom's heart was thudding, loud against his ribs. Demons were half blind and half deaf—but they were very close, now. The blackthorn was quivering with the tremors of their footfalls.

One of the demons stretched out a heavy arm. It snatched a branch out of its way and the whole tree heaved and whipped back and Tom's feet slipped. He fell, grabbed, caught something, and hung.

He'd set the birds squawking—but the demons didn't even turn their heads. They trudged on, half deaf, heedless. By the time Tom had found a foothold again all that was left of them was the ugly blaring of their voices.

Tom drew in a long slow breath and gave thanks to all the stars.

A ruffle passed over the clearing—not much more than a stirring of the leaves—and the Tribe was there again before him. There were a dozen of them, cool and slim and silver-clad.

And every eye was on Tom.

On Tom, who hadn't given the alarm.

Tom took one look at them and forgot all about the demons. He threw himself down from the blackthorn, and he ran.

He didn't stop until he was through the thick belt of trees that encircled the clearing. Then he paused to listen. All quiet. No one following.

He went on again, quietly, slipping along the edge of the wood. In the mist beyond the sickly winter grass was the sprawl of the city of the demons. There were demon outposts all round the common now.

Tom turned across the grass towards an isolated tangle of thorn bushes. His nest was there. He wriggled into the lining of wool-snags and curled himself into a ball.

The Tribe had come close to discovery just then. And it had been Tom's fault.

Soon the Tribe would come and sniff him out.

Unless they chose to make him wait.

He waited.

2

The clouds slowly darkened into tender bruises and nothing came near Tom except a chaffinch, which sat and preened itself on a branch above his head. The little bird was winter-thin, nothing but bones and feathers, but—

Tom arranged himself carefully.

One. Two. Three.

Now!

He lunged and grabbed. His sleeve got caught on a bramble, but he managed to catch hold of a handful of needle-sharp claws and suddenly the chaffinch was flapping and fighting for its life. It scratched and pecked and screamed, twisting in his cold fingers. Tom hastily wriggled his other hand up through the branches so he could wring its neck: but it was too late. The bird squirmed and scratched its way to freedom, and Tom was left holding three bloody feathers.

He sucked the blood mournfully off the quills. The hillside was ringing with acid alarm calls, now: every creature on the alert. That put paid to any chance of his catching anything—but then there had never been much chance. Tom sighed. No chance of food tonight. Unless he gave himself up to the Tribe.

The winter wind was shrinking his flesh. He shivered and wavered and hugged himself. The Tribe would take revenge on him if he went back—but there was no escape from that, whatever he did. Not in the end.

He huddled back down in his nest. He would wait

another hour. Perhaps by then the Tribe would have drunk too deep to care much about him.

Then he would go and give himself up.

Each of the Tribe sat alone, gorging, splashed by the moonlight of the chilly night. Sia, reclining on the grass, was licking a trickle of blood from her arm. She was very, very beautiful, and she had calved Tom. That was strange, because Tom was slow, and his voice was ugly. Sia had told him so.

A stag lay among the Tribe. Its belly was split from throat to vent and it steamed, new-dead, into the air. Tom's mouth watered. He slid a foot forward into the moonlight. Every one of the Tribe saw him, but they were feeding and had no time for anything else. Tom sidled cautiously up to the body of the stag. The liver was the lowliest part of the carcass, fit only to be left for the flies— but Tom's teeth were blunt, and he hadn't grown his fangs yet. He drew his knife.

Tom ate, very quiet and still, crouched in the shadow of the stag's body.

The Tribe were pouring glinting streams of demon wine into their mouths, now. Sia's long throat was white above her silver chains. Larn sat a little way away. He was the most skilled hunter in the Tribe, and he was Tom's sire. Larn let the last of the black wine drip into his mouth and threw away the bottle. Tom shrank down even further against the warm flank of the stag.

But the Tribe were full, now, and they had attention for him.

'Tom is here,' said Sia.

Tom spoke, even though his voice was nasal and thick and they would jeer at him.

'The demons crept up on me,' he said; and he was surrounded by cold high laughter.

'Demons, creeping?' asked a voice, with scorn.

'He must be as blind as a hedgehog.'

'He's as hoarse as a hedgehog.'

'And deaf.'

'And *careless*.'

At that the laughter left them.

'We were nearly discovered,' said someone. 'That must never happen again.'

'He must be taught to stay awake.'

'And he must remember.'

Tom waited.

Then someone said:

'Give him a prod with a spear.'

Tom covered his face with his arms. That was all he could do.

He waited.

The frost creaked as someone came close. Tom made himself as small as he could, but a hand yanked his belt and he instinctively put out his hands as the ground came up at him. But then the grass was spinning dizzily past him and he was swinging, helpless, from his belt. The whole clearing was tumbling and waltzing and his belt was cutting into him—round and round—until he didn't know where he was or what was happening or why everyone was laughing: and then the stars and blackness swept themselves together in a giant swirl and he was flying. Flying.

He landed harder than anything he'd thought possible. For a split second he was aware of several separate things: the sting of a scratch, and the bent-under ankle, and the struggling of his beaten-empty lungs.

But then a larger pain came. It hit him with blaring demon voices and the force of a tidal wave.

His lungs were empty, so he couldn't cry out. The pain rolled over him, and swallowed him, and that was that.